These are works of fiction. Names, characters, places, and incidents either are the product of the author's imagination or are used fictitiously, and any resemblance to actual persons, living or dead, business establishments, events, or locales is entriely coincidental.

Copyright 2012 John M. McNamara
All rights reserved.

ISBN-13: 978-1475086942
ISBN-10: 1475086946

Without limiting the rights of the author under copyright reserved above, no part of this publication may be reproduced, stored in or introduced into a retrieval system, or transmitted, in any form or by any means (electronic, mechanical, photocopying, recording or otherwise), without the prior written permission of the copyright owner.

The scanning, uploading, and distribution of this book via the Internet or via any other means without the written permission of the author is illegal and punishable by law. Your support of the author's rights is appreciated.

Hunter's War

A Novella

and

Selected Short Stories

by

John M. McNamara

For Robin

John M. McNamara

Hunter's War
A Novella

1

When I first met Badger, in language school in El Paso, someone had already pinned that nickname on him. The wide face, high flat forehead and a nose so sharp it could have been fashioned from folded cardboard, made the nickname inevitable. His eyes were the clearest blue and his smile encompassed his entire face. Badger wasn't tall; he owed his imposing presence to a stocky, muscular build. When I asked about his nickname, he said it had something to do with his disposition. I never questioned that, as I never questioned much of what he told me; his manner was as reassuring as a priest's. People truly wanted to believe what Badger told them because he spoke in such a confident voice. His humor was rooted in outright deception and bald-faced lies. Granted, the butt of his humor was usually a hapless lifer…but it occurs to me now that humor was merely rehearsal for this skilled, capable liar. During my four years in the Air Force, I never met anyone who hated the military more than Badger, yet superficially seemed to cope with it so magnificently. If a practical joke could score a coup against a lifer, then Badger's zest for the prank was inexhaustible. He hated lifers…genuinely despised them. He called them flies, something someone had told him, because he said they ate shit and bothered people. A lifer's presence could transform Badger's normally jovial disposition into cloudy surliness. They depressed and aggravated him more than the war itself.

Badger recognized tiers of wars, stacked upon one another like a tower of empty beer cans. The most pressing war for Badger was waged against the lifers, demanding perseverance. But I suspect even he understood that this struggle of wills was a sham…the power of his enemies was absolute. Of all the aspects of military life against which Badger railed, lifers irked him more than any other...the autocratic command they exerted over his life. In a war zone, the greatest danger Badger feared was being absorbed by the colossal bureaucracy of the Air Force...being stripped of his individuality in the plodding march toward mediocrity. You could see that morose hopelessness pervade his consciousness, tainting his decisions. Less important than a chessboard pawn, Badger seized upon the conflict with the lifers as a surrogate for the bullets and bombs on our periphery, a war of attrition vastly different from any ever devised by Westmoreland.

The interior of the aircraft in which Badger and I flew was austere. The aircraft nose was black and elongated like a pig's snout to house antennae, giving the plane its nickname: the hog. Imagine a Boeing 707 stripped of passenger seats and replaced with a row of equipment consoles bisecting the compartment. Each of these consoles held an array of eavesdropping equipment: radio receivers, reel-to-reel tape recorders, and an intercom panel connecting the cockpit and the other intercept operators with one another. Crude equipment by today's standards...not a computer in sight. But it was state of the art hardware in 1970. There were twelve to fifteen positions in the console row, always manned, with operator redundancy built in, airmen relieving one another during the missions on the long flights. We orbited over Laos for twelve hours, and with the flight time from Okinawa, where we were stationed, a single mission could last more than twenty-four hours.

Badger sat two positions away from me, focusing on communications among surface-to-air missile crews. North Vietnam had developed one of the most complex tracking and targeting networks in the world, and the information relayed among the SAM crews as they tried to down American fighters and bombers was what Badger recorded and translated. He was skillful. Very accomplished. He could pinpoint a SAM launch, relay the information to the air mission supervisor and have an alert broadcast to all aircraft in the vicinity in seconds.

The color of everything in those aircraft was dull green, dull blue or dull gray, and the missions were thankfully as dull as the aircraft colors, consisting of long spells during which Badger and I sat, slowly scanning the North Vietnamese radio frequencies, relieving the boredom by playing battleship, whispering coordinates through the intercom until the air mission supervisor, always a lifer, cut in from his position to ask us what the hell we thought we were doing, then bark at us to get back to work. For Badger, lifers and virgins provided natural targets for his humor on those flights. A virgin was a guy on his first flight…we counted on him being nervous and a bit skittish…the perfect foil for Badger's pranks. Badger and I had perfected a routine we pulled on nearly every one of my trainees. Where Badger specialized in surface to air missile communications, I listened to tactical air communications: North Vietnamese fighters…MiGs…and their few transport aircraft. A new man in TACAIR intercept endured endless hours of ground training, listening to repeated phrases unique to TACAIR communications…simulated intercept traffic, but it could only approximate real conditions. Once airborne, the anxious trainee had to confront his fears, and those were embodied by the pride of the North Vietnamese air force: the MiG-21. The hottest pilots flew that bird…it was small, sleek as a wasp, and posed the deadliest threat to U.S. aircraft. There were no SAM sites outside of North Vietnam, and although the NVA had peppered Laos with anti-aircraft artillery, we had been assured that it was ineffective above 35,000 feet, an altitude at which we routinely orbited in an aircraft with no weapons.

During the four hours it took to reach Laos from Okinawa, I underscored my trainee's fear, relating how what veteran aircrews most feared was a flight of MiG-21s slipping across the North Vietnamese-Laotian border, ambushing the hog, and then returning unscathed to their base at Phuc Yen airfield before U.S. fighters from their bases in Thailand could react. By the time the F-4 Phantoms arrived on the scene, they would at best be able to report the site of our wreckage for the search and rescue teams. Instilling this fear was paramount in Badger's and my prank.

On the most memorable of these particular missions, my trainee, a mousy guy from New Jersey with wiry nerves, hyper as a cricket, sat beside me, scratching above his left ear and waggling his black frame glasses every few minutes. His apprehension of being aboard a combat aircraft was like a metallic scent wafting off of him. During the first two hours, he flinched every time we heard an enemy transmission. A few MiG-17s and MiG-19s were performing routine flight operations, no cause for alarm, but I never told Kessaris that. I cocked my head with each transmission, noting Kessaris' flight suit and it's darkening armpits; he was sweating despite the chill in our aircraft's cabin. I worried that the North Vietnamese would not launch any MiG-21s that day, but also reasoned that this lull in traffic, considering Kessaris' apprehension, could be beneficial. With two hours to go before we rendezvoused with a refueling tanker over Thailand, I punched in Badger's position on the intercom and asked him to babysit Kessaris while I went back to the latrine. Badger glanced down the row from his console and I winked at him. "Roger that," he replied over the intercom as I rose and motioned for Kessaris to assume my seat.

"Nothing much going on," I told him. "I'll be right back. Call Badger if something comes up." With that I unplugged my headset and walked into the aisle behind the row of consoles, but instead of going to the latrine in the rear of the aircraft, I crouched behind Badger's position and slipped him the end of my headset cord, which he plugged into his intercom jack. I could now hear what both he and Kessaris said. More importantly, they would hear everything I said.

Badger engaged Kessaris in casual conversation, asking him how he enjoyed flying, where was he from, had he found any good bars on BC Street in Koza…trying to put Kessaris at ease. I listened to them chatting with one another, Kessaris' voice calmer than when he and I had spoken earlier. The trainee was doing what he had been told, twirling the dial on one of his receivers, searching known radio frequencies for enemy traffic. The North Vietnamese air force was systematic, using the same frequencies over and over for non-critical operations, so we preset three of our four receivers to these ranges and searched for new activity on a fourth. At the moment Kessaris removed his hand from the receiver dial and stretched his fingers, Badger activated his microphone with two rapid pops. This was my signal. I placed the microphone on my headset against my throat and uttered some Vietnamese. MiG-21 pilots used a microphone strapped to their throats, giving their voices a guttural, yet still intelligible timbre. Comprehending the words took practice, but with acquired proficiency we could understand them well enough. Our microphones swung out in front of our faces on a boom attached to the headset, and someone long before me had discovered that if the boom mic was pressed against your throat, you could imitate a MiG-21 pilot with disturbing accuracy. That's how the prank was born.

I sat cross-legged in the aisle and in the language of a Vietnamese ground controller authorized a flight of two MiG-21s to take off. The relationship between a MiG-21 pilot and his ground controller was very hierarchical: the pilots obeyed what they were told to do; their actions, reflected in their communications, followed a specific pattern. Pilots requested permission for every maneuver: a change in flight heading, air speed or altitude, especially when an attack on an enemy aircraft was involved. An attack procedure required several commands, from vectoring in on the target, locking on targeting radar, arming weapons systems and eventually launching missiles. A MiG simply did not fly up behind an RC-135 without some warning. It was our job, Kessaris' and mine in particular, to plot the MiG's progress in such an attack.

Hearing my transmission, Badger asked Kessaris what was happening. We relied on Kessaris to interpret the action for Badger. The virgin said nothing and Badger reminded him to start his tape recorder, which he did, believing he was recording MiG-21 traffic on an unfamiliar frequency. A few moments later I mimicked the MiG-21 pilot reporting a successful take off and a south-western heading which Kessaris should have known would steer the MiGs toward the Laotian border. The North Vietnamese air force used a range southwest of Hanoi for air-to-air gunnery practice, so this should not have seemed like an unusual development. A few moments later I referenced my air speed…all quite ordinary, just enough of a routine to lull Kessaris. But then I went silent for a time, long enough to cause him concern. It may seem illogical, but you worry more about a MiG when you don't hear it than when you do. Badger exacerbated the unnerving silence by asking Kessaris for status updates, to which the virgin replied that he hadn't heard anything for a while.

"Really?" Badger asked. "That's not good."

I then indicated a heading change, due west, directly toward Laos. Based on the air speed I had earlier reported, Kessaris, even with his inexperience, should have guessed that I had passed the gunnery range, providing him with very good reason to worry.

Kessaris told Badger he thought he had stumbled across some extraordinary MiG activity, on a new frequency. Badger left his position and scrambled down the row to crouch next to Kessaris.

"Must be some kind of special mission," Badger said after plugging his headset into Kessaris' console.

I allowed Kessaris to stew for five additional minutes and then referenced crossing the border into Laos. This set Kessaris off like a sparkler. He called the air mission supervisor on the intercom and rapidly told him that a flight of MiG-21s had crossed from North Vietnam into Laos. The AMS, accustomed to our pranks, praised Kessaris' work and told him to keep him informed. The AMS then quietly notified everyone else at a console that a scam was in progress on position three. The joke was a squadron tradition, a legacy spanning years of flight operations…everyone had endured something similar during their training periods.

The senior linguist on the crew abandoned his position and joined Kessaris and Badger, linking his headset in with theirs. He asked Kessaris what frequency the MiGs were broadcasting on. Kessaris replied, his voice shaky, and the senior linguist wagged his head. The virgin glanced around the aircraft interior, discovering himself the center of attention, but for reasons he did not yet understand. In the dark interior of the plane the only illumination came from a single gooseneck lamp at each position, and the red and green glow from the equipment dials. Kessaris' face bore a sheen reflecting those colors.

I keyed my mic and said that I had acquired a target on my radar. The virgin immediately babbled the information to the AMS, who told him to stay calm. A few moments later I asked the mythical ground controller for permission to activate my targeting radar. Changing the temper of my voice, I responded as the ground controller and granted the pilot permission. Kessaris relayed the information to the AMS as Badger and the senior linguist discussed the gravity of the situation, wondering what the MiGs' target might be.

Then I said, as the pilot, that I had locked onto the target and requested permission to arm my weapons. Not surprisingly, the ground controller granted the request. The AMS was informed of this latest step and he asked Kessaris if the pilot had identified the type of aircraft he was pursuing. Kessaris' answer "No!" was loud enough to be heard through the aircraft. I finally asked permission to shoot down the "Yankee air pirate," but then mimicked the ground controller denying the request, instructing the pilot to approach and identify the target aircraft. Our pilot reported switching on afterburners and approaching the target, now ten kilometers in front of him. Six kilometers. Three kilometers. Visual contact established. The ground controller requested a description. With the microphone at my throat I slowly described a large, four-engine jet with a long, black nose…the hog.

"He's after us!" Kessaris screamed. "We're the target!"

Badger rested a hand on the virgin's shoulder, but he could not restrain Kessaris from struggling into his parachute, which formed each position's seat backrest. He still wore his headset, so as laughter cascaded through the plane, I uttered my final transmission: "There's a nervous Yankee air pirate from New Jersey donning his parachute, folks."

Enough of what I said registered with Kessaris that he froze. His intercom panel lit up with chatter from every other position in the row as crewmembers urged him to look out the porthole and see the MiGs. Hooting and derision. At this moment I rounded the corner and confronted Kessaris, asking him what had happened while I was in the latrine. His face, reddened by embarrassment, suddenly drained of color and he fainted. Badger guided him to his chair to prevent him from falling and when Kessaris came to, he scowled and brooded until Badger convinced him that the only true revenge lay in perpetrating the scam on the next trainee, with Kessaris playing the part of the MiG pilot. He seemed compensated for his embarrassment.

Three weeks later I had convinced a girl from a steam bath and massage parlor to return with me to my off-base apartment. While we were in bed fucking away, a sticky paste began to glaze our bodies like doughnut icing. Kessaris had convinced Badger to let him into the apartment and the wiry little shit had sprinkled powdered sugar through my bedding. Neither the girl nor I sensed it when we slid between the sheets, but as we started to sweat, the paste formed. I suppose he owed me that one.

The MiG humor was cruel, a malicious rite of passage in which we smugly exploited one another's fears, secure in our sense of invulnerability: our aircraft had never and would never be shot down. I don't know how else to explain it.

Somehow I doubt Badger would have grown as complacent as I have. When I pocketed my discharge and hurtled through the gates of Travis Air Force Base north of San Francisco in 1973, despite everything that had happened, my future seemed optimistic. Inexplicably, I was electric in my enthusiasm. I flew home to Memphis and the sapping began, a slow drain, my family and everyone around me siphoning away my energy. It's why I left.

Arriving in Wisconsin was a booster shot; my resolution returned. Another linguist, Matt Regan, as we sat waiting for our flights at San Francisco International, had extended an invitation to visit once he got settled back in Eau Claire. I bought a battered yellow Datsun in Memphis, loaded it with my few possessions and headed north on I-55 in August of 1972. Two weeks later Matt and I rented a farmhouse outside Madison…the enclosed porch was my bedroom and as autumn turned to winter the cold helped drive notions of jungle heat and humidity from my memory. When I enrolled in the university, the old idealism surged. I studied history, earned a BA and planned to earn an MA, maybe even a PhD to secure a future teaching post at a progressive campus, decrying the ills of American foreign policy under the veil of tenure. Dreams rarely stay on script. I met and married Lindsay before I graduated. Soon after she started her job at the hospital and I became, in a string of many jobs, a daytime bartender. She advanced, becoming a head nurse and now I own the bar. If it hadn't been for Lindsay, I might have gone crazy once or twice. Our marriage has never been perfect, but whose is? There were moments when it was even less than friendly, but we've made it work.

I daydream often about how Lindsay and Badger would have gotten along. Fundamentally different people, the two of them. Lindsay was an independent woman, zealous in her pursuits. But her enthusiasm for nursing waned over the years…it became just a job, like any other. Chalk some of that change up to growing older, but credit complacency for much of it. The first years together were passionate, partly because of our youth, but time brings routine, which kills vigor. If we could have skirted the tedium, then perhaps we could have maintained some excitement. Badger and I did that, kept every day exciting by making it extraordinary.

There was one instance I remember after Badger and I had moved out of the barracks at Kadena into a two-bedroom apartment just off Gate Two Street in Koza that epitomized making each day extraordinary. Okinawan architecture stressed functionality…the apartment buildings resembled prisons: concrete block, burglar bars on windows, and stairs to rooftop gardens where people grew vegetables for their tables instead of flowers. Washing was hung out to dry on the roofs. No space was wasted…an island mentality, I suppose, that sense of confinement coupled with memories of last year's typhoon. Sturdy, squat structures that seldom rose taller than three stories. They reflected the islanders themselves. Each bedroom in our apartment had a gate built into the burglar bars as a fire escape. We padlocked the gates to prevent people getting in, fearing at the same time that one night a fire would break out and in our drunkenness we would forget the lock combination.

On the night I'm remembering, Badger and about a dozen other guys were sitting around on mats and floor pillows, sipping wine and smoking a little weed. This scene had been repeated many times, and when Badger yawned, feigning fatigue around midnight and begged off, crawling to his bedroom, no one thought it unusual. He shut the door and the party continued without him for about half an hour, when someone pounded loudly on the door. That door was hollow metal, two inches thick and impenetrable. The person knocked again and the booms echoed through the small apartment. A graveyard silence fell for a few seconds and then panic exploded among the guys who were holding. They rolled up their baggies and eyed the bathroom door, debating whether or not to attempt a mass flush. The rest of us grew fearful by implication.

The next volley on the door shattered the tension.

"MPs!" someone yelled and then a free-for-all ensued. I rushed to Badger's bedroom and flung open the door. Surprise…surprise. No Badger.

And then it dawned on me. I quietly closed his door and sank to a cushion on the floor. While everyone else ran around in a panic, I heard the gate in his bedroom swing open and then close, the latch and padlock reattached. I could hear Badger giggling at the bedlam, at the crowd by the bathroom door debating whether they should flush their stashes now or try to confirm that indeed MPs had massed outside the door. They paid no attention either to me or Badger in his bedroom, where he was less than quiet until finally he swung open his bedroom door, sauntered into the middle of the room, laughing as loudly as he had pounded on the door. No one moved. They simply rooted themselves where they stood and stared at him until like a wave it washed over them. Curses spat. Anger vented. Badger surveyed the room with a panoramic glance and chortled again, chanting "Who's afraid of the big bad brother?" which eased some of the tension, but fueled the already raging fire aligning his name with practical jokes.

He never did anything in a small way. I could always count on him to inflate matters beyond reasonable proportions. He despised weakness, especially of the spirit, which was why he so hated the war, describing it as a desperate act by feeble men. "That's why it'll fail," he often said. He wasn't a brilliant man or a prophet, but he knew the war effort was doomed, could sense it from what he observed around him. Official fuckups were not jokes to him; they were evidence that he was right, and like a righteous man, he felt superior to the rest of us, playing the role of grand observer, passively absorbing all around him. He could afford his objectivity because he had made up his mind and nothing would be allowed to shake his resolve. It was the source of his calm…in the face of even the most outrageous absurdity the Air Force could perpetrate, Badger remained calm.

He and Lindsay would have had that in common. She was a cool person, never quick to anger, attributing that to her work, where no matter the disaster, she always wore a sober expression of pleasant ambivalence. Her face was long and oval, with dark brown eyes that revealed little beyond what she wanted you to see. Her hair was as dark as her eyes, pulled back in a ponytail that flipped back and forth as she moved, like a metronome giving cadence to her energy.

Back in the early 70s, when I would tell people I was a veteran, I could perceive how that statement registered with a wince or a reflexive smile meant to cover their nervousness. People's reactions fell into one of several categories: they were defensive, sympathetic, or they simply tried to avoid you. I didn't want anyone's sympathies then; I was sick of avoidance and was the one who most often became defensive. I blundered through situations, entrusting people with confirmation of their preconceptions. I was more than just a little eccentric…even dangerous. Call me elitist, but most of the people I've met are fairly ignorant, as insensitive as cattle. It didn't take much provocation for my vitriol to seep out in those days.

Lindsay always said I was far too sarcastic, far too often, and she rarely ducked an opportunity to remind me of her opinion. Had she known me when Badger and I roamed the bars on BC Street, she might have softened her judgment. Badger wasn't a drinker…alcohol was a lifer's distraction…but he habitually accompanied me when I sought that sweet numbness. He named himself the "voice of reason," and when I sprawled in a bar booth before a tabletop foamed with spilled beer, he would guide me outside, prop me against a wall and whisper that the "voice of reason" counseled we retreat to our apartment. He would steer me toward a taxi, ignoring my acerbic rants, and direct the driver to the apartment.

    Badger tried to change my nickname once. The U.S. launched drones over the North to take reconnaissance photos and codenamed them "Buffalo Hunter." Joseph Hunter…Buffalo Hunter. Badger called me Buffalo for more than a week, but it didn't stick. The Beatles song "Get Back" had a line: Jo-Jo was a man…whatever. The song was popular when we were in language school, and as the only Joseph in a class of sixty airmen, Jo-Jo artlessly evolved. In a bar we frequented in Juarez that served shots of tequila for a dime apiece, we'd feed quarters into a jukebox and obnoxiously sing along with the lyrics. Jo-Jo it was, and Badger had to settle for being the only nicknamed animal in our group.

    Lindsay and I were so fortunate that we were not married then. Each day brought a little more pressure to bear on the marriages of men I knew. We watched them disintegrate, one by one; as individual control of lives eroded, marriages lost cohesion. Airmen's wives found their reserves of tolerance and understanding strained. Most found themselves during those first crucial years of marriage, when learning to adjust to one another would be difficult enough, coping (if you were lucky enough to accompany your husband overseas at your own expense, which many could not afford) in a foreign country, isolated from your family and surrounded by strangers, sitting in a tiny apartment, waiting for those moments when your husband could be home. The only friends you made were other airmen's wives; you forced yourself to like them because there was no one else, and you fended off the constant come-ons from your husband's friends when he had to work a night shift. Every month or so he packed a bag and flew off to Cam Ranh Bay in Vietnam for three weeks while you worried, alone, about his safety in a war zone.

Many marriages simply couldn't defy those odds. People I knew to be happily married before leaving El Paso arrived in Okinawa and experienced an evaporation of happiness. If you watched closely, you could chart its decline. Leaving your wife in the states and wondering what she was doing seemed equally frightening to some. I am so very glad I did not have to worry about cementing together a marriage during those years. It was difficult enough when I got back.

Badger swore he would never marry, but I think with his love of argument he would have enjoyed marriage. Confrontation, polarization and opposition were his anthems. It might have been a weakness, but he always dealt with people as extensions of their labels. Everybody had a tag and he filed them under those headings. He never told me if he settled on a tag for me and never gave a clue if he established one for himself. As the jester in our comic little war, he cracked jokes around officers…military royalty…each quip a spiked barb of truth. Not like Lindsay. I won't say she was humorless, but she tended to the serious side and that caused problems with us early on. We argued a lot and it didn't matter about what…important issues, trivialities… every instance held the potential to bloom into a full-blown fight. I'd tread a fine line around her, trying not to waiver to either side, which was like committing a grievous wrong. That would bring aggressive criticism and I would retaliate, lashing out to undercut her ability to hurt me. There was only one person who could hurt me more than Lindsay and that was me.

When I think back to our early months of discovering one another, I am amazed at the shared dreams and hopes, how our ambitions fit together like fingers lacing into a fist. We were happy and believed our futures would be linked forever. Naïve, to a degree, but it didn't diminish our idealism, and even time only slightly tarnished it, rubbing thin the veneer until we saw what lay beneath: nothing much to inspire confidence in one another. For a stretch we mechanically marched through our lives like inadequate actors in a play, delivering monotonic lines and stiff stage motions, but lacking any heart. The only audience we seemed to impress with our deficiency of passion was ourselves.

I could never complete a discussion of Badger with Lindsay. She never understood, even though at moments I sensed she wanted so desperately to console me. She couldn't put form to the pain she was trying to assuage...as a healer that frustrated her immensely...and then I blamed her for not exorcising my demons. That was never fair of me. I lost faith in the two of us as an us, but she stuck by me when the bulk of my resume listed previous employment, when boredom or the feeling of being cramped or restricted drove me to break out of jobs as though they were prisons. She persevered at her career and was careful never to lord her reliability over me. We accumulated a home and new cars...all the middle class accoutrements enjoyed by our parents...while I ignored her need for security. While Lindsay planned I barely worried about tomorrow, much less next week.

That was how Badger and I lived. Surviving the war, and the Air Force, was our only imperative. One day at a time. There were no weekends or weekdays...only today, every morning without fail. Time passed too slowly to plan for a future. You sensed that if you dwelled on the future it would never arrive. The only sensible approach was to let the future sneak up on you, like a parent and young child playing hide and seek. The parent closes his eyes and knows where the child is hiding, but furthers the illusion, counting out loud despite the giggles that give away the child's position. And when the child charges home base, you keep your back turned until the last possible moment and then lunge for home base a split second behind the child. You let the child win or you lose.

2

Badger preferred Vietnam to Okinawa. He enjoyed running the beach at Cam Ranh Bay and welcomed the reprieve from authoritarian enforcement of the rules and regulations that plagued us at Kadena. He also enjoyed flying the RC-130s more than the RC-135s; on the RC-130s there was only one lifer per flight, and the guy was more prone to overlook matters like haircuts and uniforms, so he volunteered for as many TDYs as he could manage. The things of paramount importance to us then of course seem so petty now. The schedule at Cam Ranh was much more relaxed, with only one flight every third day. In between missions the time was mostly our own and we spent it on football, sunbathing, smoking dope and watching movies at the outdoor theater, which was a zany place. There once had been a plywood screen attached to the mailroom wall, with bleachers facing it like an amphitheater. A typhoon totaled the screen one season and it was never repaired, so the projectionist simply showed the film on the side of the building, which was constructed of corrugated metal. Every three inches the film image dipped and rose like corduroy. It wasn't too awful if you arrived early, just before dusk…you could sit directly facing the wall, but if you arrived any later, you were forced to sit off to the side, where the visual effect of alternating vertical strips of overlapping images was boggling. In addition, at some time during the showing, one or two armored personnel carriers would rumble up behind the bleachers, shaking those rickety structures, coughing out exhaust as the drivers maneuvered the vehicles into a position from which the crews could also watch the film. The engines overwhelmed all dialogue momentarily and then hatches would crank open and four to six armed soldiers would emerge, perching on the armor plating, popping cans of beer, the crackles of their radios occasionally making heads turn their way.

Herky Hill drive-in. That's' what we called the theater, named for our barracks location. The C-130 Hercules was our aircraft and everyone on the Hill has some connection to the aircraft...and we were all transients, temporary assignments at Cam Ranh. We linguists were from Okinawa, there were loadmasters from California and South Dakota, flight crews from the Philippines and Japan. You never knew who you might meet on the Hill and where he might be permanently stationed.

One flight crew of young lieutenants from Japan developed a high-spirited reputation for unmilitary bearing. Flights suits at that time had Velcro-backed nametags you could easily remove for laundering. When this flight crew was assigned to Cam Ranh, they called themselves the Fucker Brothers. As soon as they boarded their RC-130, they removed their issued nametags and replaced each one with a new one bearing their actual first name, but the last name Fucker. They were a blast. They didn't mind if you came up to the flight deck, and if you were lucky enough to find the pilot or co-pilot sacked out on the deck, you would often be invited to sit in his seat. One time after a mission, when we were flying down the coast of South Vietnam, Michael Fucker, the pilot, let me sit in the co-pilot's seat and fly the aircraft for half an hour. I banked into slow turns and glided into a shallow dive. It was a marvelous experience.

An even more enviable bonus to flying with the Fucker Brothers was a night in Thailand. Missions flown out of Cam Ranh landed in Udorn, Thailand to drop off the recordings of intercepted traffic for transcription by guys on the ground there. We never understood why the Air Force didn't make us transcribe our own tapes…we flew out of Cam Ranh every third day and spent the rest of the down time on the beach, idle and stoned. An idle airman is not an ideal airman; busy work is the sacrament of every good lifer.

When you flew with the Fucker Brothers, you had an excellent chance of watching them manufacture a night in Udorn. Once we landed and passed off the bag of our audio tapes, the Fucker Brothers pilot or co-pilot engineered the "ground crew stall," alerting the maintenance chief about a "malfunction" of the aircraft. The system in question would be located in a relatively inaccessible part of the aircraft, requiring hours of disassembly before the pilot could be assured of the system's working order. While the ground crew sweated in the steamy heat, the air crew lounged in an air-conditioned restaurant, eating steak sandwiches and tossing money into a pool, guessing during which quarter hour period the decision to layover rather than return to Cam Ranh would be made. Compared to Cam Ranh, Udorn was a theme park with hookers. Bars, vermin-free beds, and lovely, lovely women. The crew would bus into town, splinter off into smaller groups and escape into the many distractions, often reveling until dawn. The following morning, hung over and weary, we boarded the bus back to the air base, shuffled onto the aircraft and attempted to sleep on the flight back to Cam Ranh, hoping the pilots didn't plow the damned thing into a mountainside…they never seemed any better off on those mornings than the rest of us.

The Fucker Brothers were a desirable and predictable occasion. You learned a day or two in advance when you would be flying with them and so packed a small bag with jeans and a shirt, and you traded military pay certificates on the Herky Hill black market for some U.S. currency or Thai baht. Our aircraft were never subjected to customs inspections when they returned from Thailand to Vietnam, so some guys bought gold in Thailand and sold it back in Cam Ranh.

As far as Vietnam service went, Cam Ranh was a safe place. One time the Viet Cong rocketed the flight line while Badger and I were there. I don't want to talk about that right now. The only other time I felt vulnerable was when I lost my wallet at the outdoor theater. Besides my ID there wasn't much in it that had to be replaced. The First Sergeant said to report to the base's main gate to have a new ID made. From Herky Hill I rode a bus with windows shielded with chicken wire, designed to deflect any hand grenades someone might have wanted to toss into my lap. We rode along the coast, over sand dunes…sand was everywhere at Cam Ranh…and finally along a road leading to the main gate, to a complex of low, sand-bagged buildings, concertina wire and armed security guards. Long, single-file lines of Vietnamese waited to enter the base. The bus stopped a quarter mile from the gate and dropped me off. I wore my flight suit and sweat had already darkened the neck and armpits. Trudging down the sandy asphalt, I experienced my first fear at being in Vietnam. The only ground I'd touched in Vietnam had been air bases…Cam Ranh, DaNang, Phu Bai…all air bases. But as I neared the front gate, I reflected on the world that lay beyond it, where the war was being fought. I had never been palpably afraid before that moment, not while flying, not in the barracks at Cam Ranh at night, not when we roamed up and down the beach past the barbed wire and the bunkers. But when I approached the main building and spoke to an airman with his M-16 slung over his shoulder and hand grenades strapped to his webbing, the situation crystallized for me in a way it had not before.

He directed me to the front of a long, plywood hall. Vietnamese were everywhere, carrying bundles, bags and boxes. I imagined each contained a bomb. The irony of so many of us who spoke Vietnamese existing in such isolation from the Vietnamese people was not lost on me then. A couple of old, toothless women cleaned our barracks and cleaned our laundry. If you spoke Vietnamese to them, they cackled in shrill tones to one another until you walked away. But the people at the gate were younger, stronger, and I thought, more fearsome. Remembering news stories of terrorist bombings, I felt my fear escalate and my perspective narrow. I remember as I watched all those people how frightened I was by the finality, the void created by death. I walked to the front of the hall, eyeing every face in the crowd, studying each of them, scrutinizing every weary movement, slogging through absolute paranoia that one of them would hurl a grenade or satchel charge near me. I reached a booth with three plywood walls, in which rested an old piano stool looking totally out of place. Facing this enclosure was a weighty camera on a tripod. A young sergeant with a handlebar moustache sat me on the stool, loaded the camera with a Polaroid film pack and then clicked the shutter release. While we waited for the picture to develop, he flirted with some girls standing in line. I stood with my back against the wall. When the sergeant stripped the backing off the photograph, he laughed. The camera had framed me beautifully, from the neck down to my waist. He explained that he hadn't adjusted the camera from its usual position for photographing Vietnamese workers. "Always need to tilt it up for Roundeyes," he'd said. But instead of adjusting the camera, he twirled the piano stool until as I sat my knees pressed against my chest. The next shot developed well, so I signed my new ID, watched him laminate it and then hurried out of the building. My nervousness didn't dissipate as I walked along the road to the bus stop…I was still the tallest and whitest person in a line of people coming on base for their day's work.

Any grunt would have laughed at me had I told them that was the first time I had actually been afraid during that war. I flew over the damned war, had never seen a firefight, had never buried my head in mud to keep it from being blown off. That day, as unlikely as getting a new ID card might seem, galvanized the war for me. Fear has a way of doing that, I suppose, bringing into focus what's important.

Badger, of course, laughed when I related my fear to him. He joked about everything.

When we flew night missions, there was very little to do, especially for Badger and me. Even the war seemed to sleep. We'd listen to Australian radio…reception is fantastic at 30,000 feet…or sit a pair of trainees at our positions and grab some sleep. Occasionally we'd stand at a hatch and study the ground, a dark landscape dotted with tiny pockets of glowing light. They weren't villages or VC camps. One lifer told us they were phosphorus deposits uncovered by repeated air strikes. Laos, during the day, defied even clichés of how the bombing had defaced the land: lunar landscape, like a pizza, rampant acne scars. What vegetation couldn't be blasted from the ground was defoliated. It wasn't a lunar landscape, it was a man-made warscape and it resembled nothing. Raze a building, even an entire neighborhood and you can't replicate the effects of intensive bombing. It is an awesome and striking site, not devoid of a twisted beauty.

Badger joked with new guys that the B-52 carpet bombings, which we could watch from those same hatches, had one purpose only: strip mining the phosphorus because the Army needed the element for flares and ammunition. It stunned me how many swallowed his humor without questioning him. He was the most accomplished liar I knew. Liar may seem too strong a term, but he was an uncanny con-man. He could hook more unsuspecting listeners than I ever would have thought possible. People were willing to believe him I suppose because what they saw happening around them seemed so surreal that nothing, however bizarre, could be placed outside the realm of the possible. One glimpse of the Laotian landscape and you were primed to suspend your disbelief. Given enough time, anything could happen.

Reminiscing about the Fucker Brothers reminded me of the time Badger and I dabbled in international smuggling.

The two of us were TDY at Cam Ranh, and dope stashes were running low. About two weeks into a three-and-a-half week assignment, Badger and I found ourselves slated to fly with the Fucker Brothers. We learned they were about to rotate back to Japan after this flight and had not yet overnighted in Udorn on their current TDY. We prepared for a layover and hoped the Fucker Brothers would not disappoint us. The flight proceeded uneventfully and as we banked into the landing pattern at Udorn, Badger and I crossed our fingers in hopes that we'd spend the night in Thailand. We passed off the tape bag, disembarked and wandered through the small terminal building toward the restaurant and then waited. The Fucker Brothers gave no indication that they wanted to spend the night, and we wondered if our plan would die there on the runway. But an hour later, the air mission supervisor ordered a beer and we knew: no lifer would order a beer if he was going to fly. Badger and I left the restaurant and returned to the flight line: the aircraft was gone! We walked out further on the tarmac and saw it being towed to an empty revetment. Returning to the restaurant, we found the Fucker Brothers bitching because the plane was inoperable. I couldn't believe it…their chagrin was genuine. This was not one of their customary snow-jobs; it was a legitimate malfunction. The Fucker Brothers had not intended on laying over, they were unprepared for the delay.

When they notified the rest of the crew of the situation, they were visibly embarrassed, forced to borrow money for hotel rooms. Badger loaned the pilot twenty dollars…more than enough for a room, dinner and a girl. When the AMS inquired about when the aircraft would be repaired, the crew chief said a week. The crew cheered…a week in Udorn! But the enthusiasm bottomed out when the pilot said the entire crew would return to Cam Ranh the following day when the next flight dropped off its tape bags. Yet, we had a night!

We sank into the bus seats, no wire cages in Thailand, and allowed the wind to baste us during the half hour ride to the Royal Hotel. Everything in Thailand seemed royal…hotels, bars, massage parlors. The king and queen were popular with the people. When we arrived, Badger didn't wait to check in, he flagged down a samlo, a bicycle rickshaw contraption, and told the driver he wanted to buy some ganja. We sat in the pedi-cab in our sweaty flight suits, our helmet bags in our laps, and that old brown man pedaled down the muddy streets, and when the traffic seemed most precarious, he turned to chatter to us in fractured English. Fifteen minutes later he stopped before a small shop, set in a row of similar storefronts. A ditch ran along the road, the stench repellent in the heat, with a metal grate spanning it. The driver motioned for us to go inside, then sat back on his seat and lit a cigarette. Badger and I got out, our flight suits sticking to the leather seat, crossed the short bridge and walked into the front room of the shop.

An elderly man with a gray goatee greeted us, a velvet pin cushion strapped to his wrist. Bolts of cloth lay stacked on shelves and on a high table in the center of the room. He bowed and said something to us in Thai. The samlo driver yelled to the old tailor and he smiled and bowed again, gesturing for us to follow him through a set of heavy drapes which separated the front room from a long, narrow room behind it. There, at a wide low table sat four young girls, each one wielding a cleaver on a chopping block, cutting dope and weighing it on an old set of scales. As we entered, the tailor barked and the four girls stood and bowed toward us, their hands clasped before them in a prayerful manner. I bowed slightly but could not take my eyes off all the marijuana on the table, more than I had ever seen in one place. Through gestures and head bobbing, Badger dealt with the old man and five minutes later the two of us stuffed ten one-pound bundles of Thai Red into our helmet bags. Each pound cost five dollars. Five dollars! The same pound sold for fifty dollars back in Cam Ranh. I could not believe it. The old man followed us out to the street where our samlo driver napped on his bicycle seat. The tailor called out to the driver and he woke, immediately smiling, eager to pedal us to the Royal Hotel.

Badger and I rested our helmet bags on the floor of the samlo, and I started to grow apprehensive on the return trip. At every corner I assumed a Thai policeman would leap forward and arrest us. We tipped the driver two hundred baht, about ten dollars then, and the fellow seemed grateful as hell, insisting he serve as our nightlife guide that evening, that he knew all the best places to party. By now my flight suit was dripping wet…the product of the heat and my anxiety. I told Badger I didn't want to go out that night and leave all our stuff in the hotel room, but he merely ignored my objections and told our driver that after we'd showered, we'd want to go to a good restaurant for dinner and then take a little tour of some clubs. The two agreed on a time and the man pedaled away. Badger clapped me on the back, told me I was sweaty as hell, and admonished me not to worry. As we registered for a room, some of the other crew members met us in the hallway and asked us where we'd gone. They couldn't have known what we'd been up to, but the way they looked at us made me think they knew. Badger laughed, said something about urgent business that just couldn't wait, then gripped his crotch with his hand. The others laughed and strode down the corridor. I imagined they could read my guilt in my sweat stains. Once in the room I was beyond nervousness…I was developing a healthy sense of panic as the import of what we were going to do the next day began to sink in on me. I stared at my helmet bag, then picked it up and opened it. There lay my five one-pound bundles, neatly wrapped in sheets of Thai newspaper. Bars of gold would not have they impressed me as much.

We showered and changed clothes, but when Badger said it was time to meet the samlo driver, I balked, refusing to leave the room for fear that someone would discover our cargo. Badger took me by the arm and led me downstairs, cajoling me all the way. When our driver spied us, he leapt from his seat and smiled broadly. God, but that night remains hazy to me. I had gotten stinking drunk before we left the restaurant. Thai rice wine is magnificently smooth…the taste gives no clue to the bite in it…but it rolls up on you later and your memory fails. We crawled around through several bars and picked up a pair of girls to bring back to the room. I suppose I had a good time, Badger later assured me I had, the four of us in two adjacent beds, but I can't remember it, could never swear to it.

When I came to the next day…it's not accurate to say I woke up, for I didn't feel as though I had slept…I could have died and not felt any worse. In addition to a punishing headache, my stomach felt as though it had been used as a trampoline, and when I bent over to see if my helmet bag was still under the bed, I nearly puked and came close to blacking out. Joining the rest of the crew in front of the hotel, I surveyed my friends and judged none of them looked any better than I did. Even the Fucker Brothers looked broken. They held the bus for me while I dry heaved in the hotel bathroom. We waited three hours in the terminal in a deathly silence until our flight arrived. Its crew ate lunch while the bird was refueled, but I couldn't stand the idea of food...the notion made me retch. Eventually we all scrambled on the aircraft and settled in for the three-and-a-half hour ordeal to Cam Ranh. I slept part of the way, as much as you can sleep on an airplane, more a sense of drifting off into nothingness. I sweated some more into my already rank flight suit and my hangover shifted into high gear. The drone of the propellers seemed my personal penance.

When the RC-130 began its descent into Cam Ranh, I almost couldn't bear the waiting any longer. I entertained fantasies of the plane crashing and the recovery teams finding me crumpled and bloody beside my intact helmet bag bursting with smoking marijuana. But we landed routinely and taxied along the tarmac...right past our squadron staging area, where we always parked and disembarked. The aircraft continued rolling right up to the sprawling passenger terminal. You must realize that at this time in history, Cam Ranh Bay housed the busiest airport in the world. I about shit myself. It's true what they say: fear has a metallic taste and it breeds in a dry mouth. I was prepared to surrender myself and my contraband to the first person of authority I saw, but Badger treated the diversion as just one more adventure. He whistled and said he saw some security policeman approaching the plane...they had dogs with them. Just then the air mission supervisor said there would be customs forms to fill out. It was all wrong! We never completed customs forms, but outside the plane stood two SPs with German Shepherds.

The AMS distributed the forms. In one section it asked me to list what I had to declare. I was tempted to write "Five pounds of Thai Red," "Massive amounts of stupidity" and accept the consequences of what I had done. Badger said he had nothing to declare at the moment but that the doctors might find something in a few days. This brought half-hearted laughter from the others, all of whom seemed to be feeling the brunt of their hangovers as badly by then as me. The AMS collected the customs forms, went to the hatch and handed them to the SPs, who then turned and sauntered away. The pilot taxied back to the squadron area and killed the engines. Badger looked at me, sitting stupefied and silent. We debriefed in the Quonset hut that served as our headquarters building, checked in our equipment, and rode the bus back to Herky Hill.

Back in our room, Badger and I removed the packages from our bags and laid them out on our beds. "Ten pounds," he said. Then he started doling out the dope into coffee cans; it all fit into four cans. "Deal in bulk when you can," he said.

At around five that evening, running solely on aspirin and soda, we started walking along the beach road toward the far side of the base, where a friend who had been with us in language school but had flunked out was stationed. We carried three of the cans with us, leaving the fourth on the Hill for personal use. We'd been hiking along for about twenty minutes, it was about a two-and-a-half mile trek, when an SP Jeep pulled up beside us and a huge black sergeant asked us what the fuck we thought we were doing. No explanation seemed to satisfy him as he asked for our IDs and ordered us into the back of the Jeep. Badger smiled as he climbed in, nestling his helmet bag between his legs and started bullshitting with the guy and his partner. He asked what was happening and the sergeant said the base was on Yellow Alert and we were prohibited from walking around. Badger feigned surprise, explaining we'd only returned from Thailand that afternoon and hadn't been told about the alert. The SP's partner said "Tough shit" and that we would be taken to SP headquarters until someone from our unit could come and get us the next morning. I wanted to scream, to jump from the Jeep and sprint toward the ocean, swimming for hours if need be to avoid sitting in the rear of that vehicle. But the black SP said "No shit, man! Thailand! What part?" He and Badger started talking about Udorn and the great time we'd had there, the drinking, the women, how hung over we'd been on the flight back. And the black SP said "Shit, man! I gotta get to Thailand soon! Get me some R&R and go to Bangkok. That's a great name for a city, man, Bang Cock!"

He and Badger were warming to one another, and when we turned off the beach road, he asked Badger where our friend's barracks was. Badge grinned at me, gave the barracks number and sat back, smug, so damned smug. They drove us to within a hundred yards of the barracks, returned our IDs and admonished us to stay off the streets until morning. Badger thanked the guy and waved to him as they drove away.

Badger had that way, that touch with people, an ability to connect and to wiggle his way out of or into whatever situation he chose. I felt slight and insubstantial by comparison.

My god! International drug smugglers. I haven't the nerve to attempt anything like that now. I barely managed it then.

3

I realize I bitch about it…bitch about it constantly, though not as much anymore to Lindsay…but I believe I am more content with my life now than I was then. I seem to need a routine before I can feel in control. Not in charge…just in control. There's a distinction between the two which is important to me. I need to be able to walk away from a situation…which may explain my uneasiness about marriage, although with Lindsay I've never been more in control in my life. We've placed an emphasis on mutual independence and not on individual power. I never wanted to be in a position, like some lifer, to dictate to others, and I damned sure don't want anyone else, ever again, dictating to me. I cherish the freedom to walk away from my situation if it ever sinks that low again. I'm fierce about that. If you back me into a corner and leave me with nothing left to lose, then we are going to battle. I won't swallow that line of bullshit again.

Early in our marriage I worked in a bar, and I enjoyed it. I established a routine for myself. It wasn't boring but the excitement wasn't going to drive me to an early grave either. It was an ordinary, neighborhood bar, located on a corner, with regular daytime customers who never got unruly, but calmly sat and watched the television mounted in the corner of the bar. The owner had never spent much money on the furnishings: a plywood bar painted black and red, covered with worn Formica. The checkered black and white floor so worn you almost couldn't detect the pattern of the tiles, concrete showing through in a few patches. Mostly the décor kept curious people who roamed in from the street from overstaying their welcome. It was the sort of place you don't go to unless you'd been there before…no flashy neon beer signs, no jiggling waitresses…dollar draws then and a bartender with a smile.

One regular I remember, an older woman who carried around a lot of stuff in an old paperboy's canvas bag…Caroline I think her name was, wore enough makeup to camouflage an infantry platoon… waddled in every afternoon and downed two Scotches. I usually paid for one of them; she was steady and predictable. We'd talk for an hour or more about nothing of consequence and then she'd leave. I looked forward to seeing Caroline every day. She was optimistic for someone who had no reason to be.

One day she sat and we chatted and just before she gathered her cigarettes from the bar and got ready to leave, she paused. We had been talking about marriage; she told me a bit about her dead husband and also about her son, a janitor who suffered from a learning disability and had just the day before declared that he wanted to move out of the apartment the two of them shared to move in with a woman he works with. Caroline asked me if I loved my wife. The question stung a bit. I didn't tell her it was none of her business: Caroline and I can afford honesty with one another because there's no investment between us. Nothing's lost if one of us steps on the wrong nerve.

I don't know why it's so easy for me to reason out why I love Lindsay, or why I fell in love with her: her serenity, a calm unlike any I have ever encountered before; she weathers everything …nothing seems to ruffle her, and believe me, I've tried. She tolerates me… obvious to anyone who knows us. Never underestimate the magic of tolerance. It is the basis, the requisite foundation, of so many successful relationships. Like friendship, a tacit understanding between two people to use one another in a bond that you prize. Lindsay and I were the best of friends before we married. We used each other then and we tolerate one another now, although she tolerates me more than I need to tolerate her. It is a two-way street. From that focus we expand, from friendship to love to tolerance.

I know I'm selfish, but I try to give of myself as much as I can, and I try to be less self-interested than others, even though I still look out for number one. The Air Force preached collectivism and condemned individualism, so to survive, I and everyone I knew became more self-centered, overcompensating to retain our own identities. Some overreacted and the system, ironically, singled them out and punished them. Skip Balfour, who was in language school with Badger and me, roomed in the barracks in Okinawa down the hall from us. The first day he was scheduled to report for duty at Torii Station, he stayed in his bunk. Skip refused to get out of bed. He ignored messages from the first sergeant for two days until two security policemen showed up and carried him from his bunk, in his underwear, to the squadron commander's office. I didn't see it, but several guys did and we listened to them describe it in detail that evening. Skip told the colonel that what the unit was doing was just wrong and that he would have no part in it. He never elaborated and the colonel never asked him any questions. No threats, no intimidation. That afternoon Skip was placed on a plane back to the states, with an SP escort. His roommate heard from him about a month later from North Dakota…he was a cook's helper there until he was discharged. They took his stripes and reduced his pay, but he never spent any time in the stockade and he stayed out of the war; well, to a degree, but if not out of it, well away from it.

Badger and I used subtlety to maintain our identities, at least in front of the lifers. I make him out to be the world's most flagrant maverick, but for sheer survival, he could keep his zaniness out of sight of the ruling class, those idiots who found themselves in positions of authority. They ruled, but seldom had the class to do it effectively. Badger joked that all lifers had been born in Dixie...that's the only type we ever met. The Air Force, by comparison to the dirt hills of Alabama and Georgia, must have seemed awfully inviting. The power bestowed on those poor rednecks transformed them into little league dictators. Twelve years as a staff sergeant conferred on every hillbilly who donned a uniform the thread of authority to strut and screech like a world conqueror.

You can see how even today I react to all of this. Badger and I each grew up watching war movies from World War II on Saturday afternoons and playing army with kids in our neighborhoods. I always played an infantry captain who thought sacrificing his men for the sake of the country earned glory. Spill blood for the red, white and blue. God that was some strong conditioning. Every kid my age wanted to be a hero...someone honorable. War was stimulating, a game to get your blood pumping and your adrenalin flowing...to get you high! War was fun, something to anticipate, like a homecoming game. Soldiers earned respect and generated awe. So if when I enlisted in my war I was not totally anti-war, it was not surprising. I don't think I had formed any solid opinions then about the military as an organization or as a way of life. But four years of service and one war later, I can resolutely say I am both anti-military and anti-war.

Enlistment...coercion is a more accurate description. I remember the day I walked home from unsuccessfully trying to register for classes at Memphis State University to have my father greet me at the door, wearing an implacable, serious look on his face. He pointed to the mailbox and said there was a Selective Service notice in it. My grades the previous semester had cost me my student deferment. Serving in the infantry, but not as a captain, seemed a possibility then. Among my options, I succumbed to the one which seemed less dangerous: enlisting in the Air Force. I felt I could weasel a job as some sort of clerk in Germany, far from Southeast Asia. During the enlistment process, I completed a series of tests, one of which measured my aptitude for languages. In basic training I was assigned to Vietnamese language school…more of the fresh meat headed to the grinder in Vietnam.

So I am anti-military and anti-war and that may be anti-reality… after all, there will always be wars and armies. We've just ended a decade in which the world has spent more money on combined military forces than in any other time in our history. We still glorify soldiers to our children, hammering the adventure and allure of war through video games…calling them to duty. The structure still depends on the blind loyalty of eighteen-year-olds, whose minds are still malleable, who are still susceptible to domination, who haven't yet developed a sense of self strong enough to mount any resistance to indoctrination. Every tyrant understands this, and so do churches. Religion snatches children early and pumps their heads full of that special brand of truth: the divine propaganda of God's chosen ones, who are able to spew hatred because someone's race, gender or discredited beliefs just somehow don't measure up. They breed lifelong disciples. It was virtually impossible to attend a state university before the 1960s without being required to attend ROTC classes. Breed those warriors! I read a newspaper article the other day…ROTC enrollment, which had been increasing before our forays into Iraq and Afghanistan, is now tapering off. Whereas recruiters used to say that young people hadn't heard of Vietnam, today they watch video of our current wars and balk at enrolling in the many ROTC classes on campuses across the country. It makes me hopeful, even though we are a country with a short memory. Everything seems so unbalanced. War fever burns through the country and high school kids can't wait to graduate because they're afraid the war will end before they can grab a taste of it. But once the war sends home the body of a friend, when the grinder revs up, feeding on our young men again, then the country, once propelled by arrogant pride, allowing it to so easily march its sons and daughters to war in some twisted sense of vicarious fulfillment, well, then the country rebels, and deems those sacrifices too dear, too costly. But that judgment is always so slowly made. Then the men who seek vicarious fulfillment through their grandchildren's sacrifices will have to look elsewhere to establish their destructive legacy.

We are such a goddamned violent nation. We seem to revel in it, to glorify it, and when we find ourselves on the wrong side of history, we revise it, transforming the past into a tribute to our righteousness. We revere ignorance in this country. We truly do. We never recognize patterns, repetitions of mistakes. I feel so powerless when I see this vicious cycle cranking up all over again. And angry, so fucking angry at how no one listens. I wonder if it's always been this way. My anger can't be that unique.

Although I'm unsure now, I once believed everything in my life tied together somehow. The resentment I sometimes feel for Lindsay because she cannot understand what I'm saying. She tries, I know, but she cannot imagine my experiences. The old adage: you had to be there, right? Maybe that's why I took so many lovers…and always neutral women. I asked little of them and offered even less. Was it any surprise that I expected so little from them in return? The affairs, as affairs go, were very safe: no expectations, no disappointments. Nothing revealed and no involvement beyond the superficial. Lindsay, however, is another matter. Our intimacy bridges several layers, so she is more of a threat. I guard against what she could do to me and feel defensive a great deal of the time. Lifers made me feel the same way… the conditioning, never growing too close, maintaining your distance.

I'm frightened because I'm getting a little too old to continue portraying the angry young man. Who succeeds the angry young man? What's the cliché that sums up the disillusioned middle-aged man? What kind of old man do I want to be?

I'm tired.

It crossed my mind that one might wonder why Badger and I never tried to get out of the Air Force. I wonder, too. We certainly hated it enough, every minute of every day, and we never pretended we were overjoyed to be where we were. But I don't remember ever giving the idea of getting out any serious consideration. We'd labor at avoiding work, at slowing down what we were doing and always maintaining a simmering surliness whenever we had to contend with lifers. But neither of us ever took the first step to get out. There were difficult procedures and we heard rumors of other who had gotten out: conscientious objectors, volunteers in drug amnesty programs. People bargained their way out but they supposedly paid for it in some unacceptable way.

One guy…Bob Pooley…attached himself to Badger and me one TDY in Cam Ranh. He was funny, smoked dope and hated lifers…all around good company. One night the three of us were playing cards in our barracks room when a lifer knocked on the door and told us the base had been placed on yellow alert. These alerts had become more and more common in the waning months, as the war wound down. Nothing much ever happened so we weren't concerned. It meant more duty for the beach and perimeter patrols, and you could bet that during the night parachute flares would light up the bay, and the machine gun bunkers near the fuel dump would squeeze off a few tracer rounds over the waves. They produced quite a light show...reminding us of how much like a game it all seemed in our relative security. Our only inconvenience during a yellow alert was being secluded on Herky Hill...the base buses didn't run. But we hadn't planned on going anywhere that night.

An hour later Badger stood to go to the dayroom for some beer but stopped in the doorway, looking north toward the hills on the peninsula. "Christ almighty," he muttered. Outside we all stared at what appeared to be a stream of molten orange metal streaming to earth. A Spooky gunship. The war crept just a little closer to us that night and the fear I had earlier felt at the base's main gate returned, rising in my throat like bad food. Pooley backed into the room. This was his first TDY to Cam Ranh and he was more frightened than the rest of us. The display lasted a few more minutes and we returned to our card game. We joked about the poor sons-a-bitches who found themselves on the receiving end of the gunfire, played for another ten minutes or so and then heard a rasping, whistling sound overhead.

None of us could identify it until we heard an explosion across the base near the flight line. Rockets. And then there were more of them arcing over our barracks as men downstairs yelled "Incoming!" as we scrambled for our helmets and flak jackets, which were crusted with dust from months of disuse. More explosions rumbled up the hill from the flight line and the ammo dumps as we huddled behind the concrete catwalks and stared. Then one goddamned huge explosion spiraled toward the clouds and Badger whispered "Daisy cutters." These bombs weighed seven-and-a-half tons and were jettisoned from cargo planes to clear helicopter landing zones in the jungle. They'd raze everything in a fifty yard radius...animal and vegetation. Some lucky VC rocketeer had scored a hit on them and the fireball from the explosion rose like a small Hiroshima. I stood rooted on the spot, couldn't move a muscle until the blast wave struck the barracks. Windows shattered, shards of glass ricocheting like confetti. My left forearm sustained a shallow cut; the scar's still there. Badger had crouched and wasn't even scratched. Pooley sprinted for the stairs like a rabbit at a dog track and was slammed against a wall, then down a flight of stairs. He landed hard at the bottom and was knocked unconscious. Badger and I dragged him to a bunker across the road from the barracks and he laid there while the VC walked their rockets away from the flight line and up the hill toward us. The three of us huddled in the bunker as a rocket exploded about a hundred yards from us. Pooley came to, muttering something I couldn't understand. Flames illuminated everything around us as Badger crawled to the bunker's entrance and peeked out, describing the whole scene. I was content to press my back against the sand bags and listen to Pooley's mumblings.

When the all-clear sirens sounded, we hauled Pooley outside and called for an ambulance, but there were many casualties that night and it was some time before the medics arrived. As we waited, Pooley sat alongside the barracks and we kept him awake, fearing a concussion or worse. He blathered, making no sense. He didn't recognize us or realize where he was. He was on a medevac flight to Okinawa the next morning.

Pooley wasn't the most serious casualty from our unit that night. A lifer, Lieutenant Tederman, had been killed. He was a retread, a bootstrapper, a former sergeant who had gone back to college and earned a degree, then returned to duty with a commission. Bootstrappers fell into one of two categories: either bastards, harsher than ordinary officers, acting as if they had been ordained by the hand of God to bring discipline to the ranks; or easy-going guys who remembered where they came from and bonded with the enlisted men out of shared experiences. Tederman had been the former, an intolerable prick who had more than a few times singled out Badger for special abuse. He'd always been on Badger's case, examining every little thing he'd done. But Badger had let it roll off his back like a cloud shadow. The night of the attack, before cards, Badger and I had walked into the dayroom, looking for some chairs to bring back to our room, and Tederman was there. His latest kick was speed-reading and he sat there speed reading a book of poetry! I don't think he understood why we laughed at him. He stopped Badger from folding up a chair and heading for the door, demanding to know where Badger was going. Badger flashed the man a "not-this-again" look and you could see Tederman's reaction immediately. Not pleased. I stood by the wall and watched. Tederman was a small man with a large skull, his hair clipped in a spiky crew cut. The sun had burned his scalp. Badger loomed over him for a moment, and you could see the frustration growing in Tederman's expression. He repeated the question and Badger merely shrugged, like there was a fly buzzing near him. He finally told Tederman he was taking the chair upstairs for a card game.

Tederman said "Don't you have a chair in your room?"

Badger said the three of us wouldn't fit in a single chair. Badger smiled as Tederman told us to bring the card game to the dayroom, which was intended for those kinds of activities.

Badger said he didn't care for the ambiance of the dayroom, that the air was old and stale, all the while staring at Tederman. Weeks prior to this Badger had asked Tederman for advice, wondering what kind of punishment could be meted out to an enlisted man who called an officer, say a lieutenant, an asshole whose mother had probably shit him out her ass rather than given birth to him. Tederman's face had turned as red then as it was turning now, and said that the enlisted man would be court-martialed for such an effrontery. Badger had slowly nodded and said "I'll bear that in mind, Lieutenant. Thank you."

Tederman glared at Badger, ordering him to return the chair, which Badger did. We left the room and Badger slammed the door. Tederman died later that night. He stumbled drunk into the path of a piece of hot shrapnel and it ripped his chest open like a jelly doughnut. There were no regrets from anyone I knew, and it didn't bother me one hell of a lot either.

But the Pooley thing; that's another matter. I still contend it was a slick con. Even when we pulled him into the bunker, it seemed his disorientation was a little exaggerated. And when I saw him back at the hospital on Kadena, I was convinced.

Badger and I left Cam Ranh about a week after the attack and when we checked in at the orderly room, learned that Pooley was still in the base hospital with amnesia. Badger didn't think it was all that unusual, but I was skeptical. Pooley, when we visited him, looked unscathed: no bruises, no cuts, no bandages. I still had stitches in my arm, but Pooley? Nothing. He sat propped up against a couple of pillows and looked at us as though we were strangers. He was robed in striped blue and white pajamas, a plastic identification bracelet on his wrist, and if he hadn't had his name pinned to him, he wouldn't have known who he was. At least that was the scam, as far as I was concerned. The three of us chatted as we walked in a grassy quadrangle on the hospital grounds; Badger didn't question the sincerity of his amnesia. I kept expecting Pooley to open up to us about it so that we could all have a good laugh, but he played it out perfectly: fuzzy memory, blurred vision that came and went, occasional dizziness. Pooley seemed to understand he was in the Air Force, that he was married and had a daughter living in Ohio. All those things were familiar to him and somehow anchored him to the earth, but he couldn't remember any word – and this was the reason I really believed it was all a ploy – he couldn't remember one single word of Vietnamese. Amnesia of a highly selective variety if you asked me. What unadulterated genius.

He remained in the Kadena hospital another week, but when his condition failed to improve, the Air Force discharged him and sent him to a Veterans hospital near his home in Akron, where a team of doctors examined him to determine his disability rating. The higher the rating, the higher the monthly check from the VA.

Green envy. That's the only way to describe how I felt on the day they loaded Pooley onto the jet for Travis. Badger and I joined some other guys from the squadron to see him off at the terminal. He was in uniform but still wore the hospital ID bracelet and carried his medical records in a blue cardboard tube. Sitting and waiting for his flight to depart was weird, because I wasn't sure what to say to him. I didn't want to blow his play-acting and the rest of the guys didn't know how to say goodbye to someone who wasn't exactly certain who they were. Pooley acted as though he understood what was happening to him, and when they announced his flight he shook hands with each of us, turned and fell into line. That's when he stopped, pivoted on the tarmac and looked straight at me. He raised a hand to his eyes, the sun was blinding, and then he winked. Badger said I was crazy. Pooley had experienced difficulty with his vision and it could simply have been dust or the sun in his eyes. But I swear Pooley winked.

Pooley forgot his way out of the Air Force. I know it. I give him points for capitalizing on the opportunity offered him. It was a first-rate con. He forgot about the war and it disappeared for him. I wonder what, if anything, he thinks about the war today.

I didn't want to have contact with anyone from those days. They're reminders of a time I want to forget, or at the least didn't want to remember. But the crying convinced me. That and Lindsay's insistence. The crying frightened me. I'd sit and watch the television, news or a movie, and if anything about the war came on, I'd begin to weep…unconsciously. I wouldn't know I was doing it until a felt the tears on my cheeks. Then I'd realize I was sobbing and Lindsay was watching me with a look of mixed pity and fear. My throat would tighten up, I'd begin to sweat, and then I'd hold my breath to try and make the tears stop. Lindsay confessed her helplessness because she wouldn't know what to say. I felt guilty making her feel helpless and then I'd feel helpless myself.

There had been a group of Vietnam vets in the mid-seventies who had begun a hunger strike of a VA hospital in Los Angeles. They wanted the VA to recognize the effects of Agent Orange. I watched CBS's report and before it was over I was perched on the end of the seat cushion screaming "Bastards!" at the VA spokesman. I cried until I couldn't any more. The next day Lindsay made me call the VA and set up an appointment with a counselor. We met on and off for a few years.

There are lapses still. But rarely. Anger dissipates quickly these days. Moods can endure, frustration that chews slowly at my mind, but I deal with it. I don't let it override everything else in my life. I don't drink any more…the alcohol only deepened the depression, and I have Lindsay to cajole me out of any lowness. She's a hell of an anchor. If I wasn't tethered to her, I don't know where I'd fly off to.

Hell, even the VA recognizes the effects of Agent Orange now on veterans' health.

4

I still don't have any tolerance for authority and I may never. Contacting the VA was the closest I've come to an act of subservience since I was discharged. But as I have already said, it was at Lindsay's urging. I held a theory back then that the VA farmed out the most troublesome cases to doctors like the one I saw. I suppose they reasoned those shrinks would represent less of an authority figure than VA staff doctors. I attended sessions voluntarily, although I was skeptical about the process and what it might accomplish. I came to respect my psychiatrist. He was fair with me and calmly demanding. He guided me through several epiphanies and for that I'm thankful.

My contempt for authority cost me some jobs and it kept me out of graduate school. Bureaucratic strangleholds extend to the academic world as well as to government and business. I can't stomach unquestioning behavior, although there are always people willing to obey unflinchingly. Trained seals balancing balls on their noses for fish. If I sound harsh, don't get the wrong idea…I can't sound harsh enough to let you know how I feel. I sought the university as a haven when I came home but it was just another balloon waiting to burst.

One of the things my shrink helped me understand was that the four years in the war stripped away everything but my thirst for ideals. With the mechanized madness whirling around me, I molded my desire for ideals into a sanctuary, elevating it beyond all reasonable proportions. When I came home and tried to practice those ideals, the house of cards that was my naiveté toppled. I anesthetized myself to obvious clues that could have warned me, could have softened my fall had I noticed them.

On the flight from San Francisco to Memphis following my discharge, there was a layover in Dallas. Passengers on the plane stared at my uniform with obvious animosity. I thought I had developed a thick skin in the Air Force, but these people caught me during a period of emotional decompression. I hadn't expected an "open-arms-welcome-home" attitude. I wasn't oblivious to the nation's mood by then, but I wasn't prepared for hostility. I changed clothes in a Dallas bathroom and threw away my uniform. It made me feel like I was sliding down a pyramid. Lindsay said going to the shrink constituted hitting bottom, then standing to start climbing up again. I'm not sure I liked her image at the time. I didn't want to climb through my past, of covering and recovering the same ground twice. That seemed too much like the pattern of the war. And I wanted to fracture the pattern, not paint in all the colors in the same numbered forms again. Lindsay said she felt it was necessary and the shrink partially agreed.

I mentioned other jobs. I worked in an office but rebelled against management…surprise. The factory had its foreman. My bar, however, is a unique setting. Within the familiar surroundings I feel secure and in control. I follow the routine I set for myself each day when I unlock the door. I rarely encounter major surprises and often go weeks without one day distinguishing itself from another.

There will always be days that set themselves apart for their history: the day President Kennedy was assassinated, the day Nixon resigned, the day the towers collapsed on 9/11. I include Badger's and my last mission among those days. Maybe that's why the smearing of one day into another now doesn't alarm me.

We flew out of Cam Ranh that day. Badger woke me and gave me an hour's warning and I rolled over back to sleep while he showered. He woke me again when he returned from the latrine and I flinched when he gripped my shoulder to shake me. The day before I'd been down on the beach playing football in the surf for a few hours and my back, neck and shoulders had sunburned. When I sat on the edge of the mattress, it sagged. Badger whistled as he dressed and I yawned, rising and stretching. My neck cramped and I felt as though I would choke. It passed and I timidly swallowed to see if the muscles would tighten again. I stood before my locker massaging my neck and examining my face in a tiny mirror mounted on the inside of the locker door. In the latrine, which always stank of mildew, I brushed my teeth and shaved. When I returned to our room, Badger was already dressed in his flight suit and his helmet bag lay at his feet. He wanted me to hurry so we could grab some breakfast at the chow hall before catching the bus to the squadron HQ. I told him to go without me but he shook his head. We skipped breakfast. He borrowed some Solarcane from the guys next door and sprayed my sunburn. It felt almost painfully cold going on but eventually dulled the pain. My flight suit chafed at the shoulders. I swallowed three aspirin with half a can of warm Pepsi and flipped off Badger as he laughed at me.

We joined the rest of the crew, ten of us in all, but I've forgotten some of the names now. There was a staff sergeant Air Mission Supervisor and seven other guys. One guy I do remember, Springer, had flown with Badger and me quite a few times, so the three of us huddled, sitting in the sand as we waited for the bus. I remember the three of us boarded last and sat in the back of the bus, not talking much, although I did comment on how the wire shielding the windows appeared to have worn out in spots and was loose where it met the window frames. We all seemed tired, more mentally than physically. When everyone filed off the bus at the HQ building, Badger joked about simply riding it back to the barracks. This occurred at five o'clock in the morning, in the dark and an uncommonly chilly air.

We trudged to the security gate, flashed our badges at the guard, and walked to the briefing room where we checked out survival vests… they were a military magician's cape: maps, matches, snake bite kits, compasses, flares and strobe lights, and a .38 caliber pistol and ammunition. Six rounds each. I always believed we'd end up shooting one another instead of the enemy should it come to that…an awfully short fire fight. There were two kinds of pistols, snub-nosed and long-barreled. The newer men always chose the snub-nosed…a reaction to watching too many movies as children. The wiser men reached for the long-barreled…they were more accurate weapons.

The briefing room was a low-ceilinged, dim room, with maps lining three walls identifying SAM and AAA sites in Laos and western North Vietnam. An intelligence officer reviewed the intercepted traffic of the past twenty-four hours. He asked that I monitor a new frequency which had been used by a flight of two MiG-21s that had approached the Laotian border the previous day, but then had veered north and returned to Phuc Yen airfield. It was unusual activity, a deviance from normal flight patterns and he wanted me to be alert for any similar activity. I nodded but said nothing. An RC-135 from Kadena would also be orbiting in the same area as we would, but at a higher altitude and farther west of the Laotian-North Vietnamese border. The RC-135 carried two TAC-ops instead of just one and they were more likely to hear and handle any such activity. I wouldn't ignore it if I heard it, and of course as it turned out I heard every goddamned word of it. But at the time of the briefing I wasn't overly alarmed by it. The North Viets didn't do it often, but they had been known to fly along the border to gauge our fighter responses.

The things we dismiss which later rise to haunt us. I've revisited my actions that day numerous times to discover if I made any mistakes in the moments before the attack, wondering if I could have been more prepared to react, not physically, but psychologically.

What the hell.

The briefing concluded and we all marched out onto the tarmac where the RC-130 was parked. The flight suit was chafing my sunburn again as low clouds diffused the rising sun's rays over the bay area in pastel colors. It really was quite beautiful. The three of us, Springer, Badger and me, moved to the steel revetment wall and slumped as the flight engineer and ground crew finished their pre-flight. Springer was a smoker and he flicked his butt down along the wall rather than step on it or field strip it. There were dozens of tiny details about the preparation for that flight and the time on orbit itself that were just slightly different than normal. But I didn't pay attention to them, although they stick out in my memory now. I've gone back and striven to remember that day more distinctly than any other. I also dream about that day, more so during my sessions with the shrink. I've seen the entire day unfold, all the insignificant details. I question if I really remember all of what occurred that day or have I allowed the years to embellish the truth, to make it a better story, or to reconstruct the events as I wish they had happened.

There have been times when I wanted to lash out and really hurt people. I like to believe it isn't in my nature, and that's why the animosity I feel toward these people who lack even the slightest bit of dignity, really distresses me. Last year at a party I ran into a guy. I don't know whether it was his mannerisms, the cadence of his speech, the tilt of his head, or the way he looked at me, but I was immediately put off by him. Within fifteen minutes I loathed him. I walked away from a conversation with him, but he pursued and cornered me in another conversation. There would be no escape I realized, so I started being wildly flippant, going out of my way to belittle him. I switched roles and became the hunter, pursuing him from circle of people to circle of people. Lindsay asked me to stop, no doubt fearing where it might all lead. I drank heavily. Sitting around a picnic table in the backyard of the host's home, I stared at the guy as he droned about his work at a downtown insurance agency and then laughed loudly in a monotone, trying to intimidate him, to provoke him. He regarded me for a moment and then continued. I brayed at him mid-sentence. He stood and walked around the table until he stood behind me. He yelled for me to get up. I sipped my drink and told him to sit down. He yelled again when I refused to face him. I slowly swiveled my head to look at him and repeated very softly that he should sit down. I wondered if I would have to fight him. His eyes were narrowed with anger and his jaw was clenched. At that moment I told him in the same sobering voice that if he forced this, if we fought in that backyard that night, I would kill him.

Lindsay rose from the table and hurried into the house.

I told the guy he would get in the first punch, but that I would waste little time retaliating, that I would be fast, dirty and would inflict a great deal of pain on him. My attack would be mortal and he ought to consider his next decision very carefully, because he seemed to me like a slow learner. It worked. He backed away from me, muttering something about the crazy fucking vet. Fine by me.

One of my old friends, also a veteran, is a pediatrician at a teaching hospital in Atlanta. When he greets his interns on their first day he tells them a story of how he became interested in pediatrics. One day, he tells them, while on patrol with his company in Vietnam, they entered a village of unfriendlies. As he and his men were dropping babies down the village well, it occurred to him that he really enjoyed working with children. I can handle that kind of humor, most vets I know chuckle at the darkness of it, but others recoil when they hear it. Some find it vulgar and Gray, my friend, says he can see the distance grow between him and those interns.

You know which senses evoke the memories of that time the most? Not the visual, but the sound and smell of it all. The pitch of the aircraft engines…an RC-130 is a propeller-driven plane, the RC-135 is a four-engine jet. Inside, the air is fouled with a metallic tang. That morning at Cam Ranh smelled briny, the wind blew slightly off the bay and when we boarded the interior air smelled just like the ocean. Springer, Badger and I all sat in the same windowless, four-man compartment. The fourth guy was named Madden; he died before he could even leave the aircraft. The engines started and the sea air was sucked away, replaced by that machine-like odor. The compartment vibrated as we took off. You can always tell the exact moment the wheels leave the runway: the aircraft, which had seemed to be rising, dips ever so suddenly, and your stomach bobs for a second or two. We backenders would never know if at that moment there was a malfunction with the plane, if after those seconds we'd continue our ascent or belly out on the tarmac in a ball of flames. I'd listen, tensed up, until I knew were climbing safely. My ears would pop as we gained altitude. There's an ancient joke about a passenger who complains to the flight attendant that his ears wouldn't pop. She gives him some gum and says it will help. At the end of the flight, the passenger thanks her but asks how to get the gum out of his ears. Every time we'd get power to our workstations, Badger would radio the AMS on the intercom and ask him how to get this gum out of his ears.

The AMS that day was Bowker, a second-term lifer who had realized re-upping was a mistake and was going to leave the Air Force after his current enlistment. He wasn't a bad guy, didn't give a shit like some of the hard-assed lifers, and did only enough to keep his butt covered from the higher-ups. We called him Bow-wow and I liked him, but to Badger he was still a lifer. A rule was a rule to Badger, as long as it was his rule. That morning Bowker replied to Badger: "Repeat, number four."

Badger repeated his punch line and Bowker said again: "Repeat, number four." Badger asked him one more time how to clean the gum from his ears, and Bowker said: "Repeat four, I'm having trouble hearing you with this gum in my ears." I could hear Bowker laughing in his compartment and even Badger smiled. Bowker survived the attack because of his position in the aircraft. He lived and Madden died…it wasn't random. If an air-to-air missile strikes an RC-130 on the right side of the aircraft, certain people will die and others will live. Madden and the guy next to Bowker, Yoste, were killed outright. The rest of us made it out of the aircraft alive.

We powered on our equipment and tested each receiver; mounted reels of tape of the recorders, and handed out handcopy sheets of water-soluble paper. Since Badger and I had missed breakfast, we headed back to the small galley to scout for food. The galley consisted of two compact refrigerators and a small oven. There were some C-rations stored in a cabinet…orange cake and caramel cake. After a few minutes in the oven, they were edible. I washed mine down with apple juice then the two of us stood by the hatch and watched South Vietnam pass below us.

We talked about Okinawa, its bars, the steam-and-creams, the girls. I had just hooked up with a new girlfriend named Emiko. She'd been dating a Marine but split when the asshole started beating her when he was drunk, which seemed to be all the time if you believed her. Emiko and a girlfriend were staying in our apartment while Badger and I were TDY to Cam Ranh, and I figured Badger could probably get the girlfriend to stay on with him when we got back. I hadn't met her, but Emiko said she was cute and not as chubby as some of the other island girls we encountered. We'd heard similar talk before, but laughed anyway. The entire crew still seemed sleepy. I thought of racking out on the floor of the compartment…a bunched up flight jacket made a passable pillow. We'd be on orbit in an hour-and-a-half and I could do with some sleep, but decided against it. Bow-wow had tuned one of his receivers to a BBC broadcast and was quietly mimicking a British accent.

There wasn't even the slightest hint that the flight would be anything but ordinary. Do you ever play the game of wondering how foreknowledge would change your actions in a given situation? Would I have flown anyway? Tried to cancel the flight? Would I have reacted more quickly once the sequence of the attack began? Or would I have remained silent until the two of us were hanging in the jungle there like limp puppets?

It's a tangle of determinism. I don't know. Even when I think of it now, I'm ambivalent. Who I am now derives so much of my identity from what happened. I am beginning to like the person I've become. It's certainly a tangle.

Any girlfriend in Okinawa was referred to as a horizontal dictionary, assuming you had any interest in learning the language. Poor joke. I met Emiko in a record shop on BC Street in Koza. She was fairly pretty, taller than other Okinawan girls. She worked at the cash register...I remember I bought Emerson, Lake and Palmer's first album. On one of its tracks was the first use of a synthesizer I'd ever heard. She wasn't a bar girl or a hooker, she was a "good girl" and there was a code on the island: good girls wouldn't date servicemen, something we all knew. I asked her to go out with me; perhaps I was encouraged because she had chatted with me when I bought the album. She seemed not only curious but knowledgeable about the States. We went to a Samurai movie and I learned she was a sword freak and that she longed to visit Japan. After she moved into the apartment with Badger and me, I toyed with the idea of taking some leave, getting on a boat and taking her to Tokyo.

Emiko and I slept together on the third date and you have to realize what a departure this was. None us really dated in the American sense...we did what we had to do to get laid. We hung out in dive bars and went broke buying watered drinks, probably ginger ale, for bar girls, who would unzip our pants under the table and play with our dicks, but still not sleep with us. You found a hooker or you went to a steam-and-cream for a "happy ending." One bath house at the end of BC Street became our last stop on many evenings when we were drunk and horny. Dim lighting, quiet music, and not a cheap place... the girls served you drinks in the soaking tub. The women were all young, strong and demure. They would strip you of your clothes, folding them neatly over a chair back, place you in a steam cabinet for a while, and then lead you to the soaking tub. Moments before you'd find yourself drifting off to sleep, your hostess would stand you on the warm tile floor and wash you all over with a soapy sponge, rinse and dry you and then lead you to the massage table. You'd first lie on your stomach while the girl kneaded the tension from your muscles. When you rolled over she'd start on the other side, and as she neared your dick, if you weren't too drunk, it would start to rise. She'd grip it in her oily hand and whisper her question in your ear: "You want special massage?" For an extra five dollar fee, which you'd scramble to remove from your wallet, she would lubricate her hand with body lotion and beat you off. One night I remember, a few of us were enjoying the ritual when we heard cackling laughter from the shared hallway. Later when all grouped outside, Badger was grinning. When asked what was so goddamned funny, he said his girl had used Brylcreem instead of body lotion and he couldn't control his laughter. "A little dab'll do ya!" he crooned and the girl had gotten upset with him because she felt he was making fun of her. She had refused to give him a hand job and he tried to explain to her that he was laughing at the Brylcreem and not her. She relented and he got his hand job.

Emiko never worked in a steam bath, but she wasn't exactly a good girl, either. I didn't know any of this until after she moved in with me. She had already split up from the Marine by the time we met; the cashier position at the record shop job was new and her friends told her he was looking for her. One night the two of us were cruising some Okinawan bars, the ones Americans rarely patronized, where prices weren't inflated by the shape of your eyes. We were in a quaint place, quiet and dark. Emiko listed Japanese words for the objects around us and the bartender, whom she knew, laughed at my pronunciation. After a few attempts I could mimic her fairly well…I was a linguist after all. Emiko managed a smattering of English, and didn't rush herself when she spoke, so we could communicate competently. We sat on stools at the end of the short bar. The lights around us shone red and Japanese pop music played from a small radio on the shelf behind the bartender. She was entertaining us, pointing to things around the room. Half the time I couldn't make out what she pointing to and when I repeated her words I couldn't always match them with the object.

 The door opened. She swiveled to see who had entered and froze. Three Americans walked in and sat at a table along the wall. Emiko faced the bartender, and then whispered something in Japanese. The bartender walked away from us as a waitress relayed the order from the table of Americans. I studied them in their mirrored reflection behind the bar: they stared at Emiko. She gripped my arm and said she wanted to go home, nearly dragging me off my stool. I was car-sitting a friend's MG and Emiko hurried toward where we'd parked it. Footsteps sounded behind us as we rounded a corner and paced down a narrow street, but I didn't turn around. I knew who was following us and they caught up to us when we reached the car. The ex-boyfriend blocked the passenger door and told Emiko he was glad he had finally found her…he'd been searching for her and who the fuck was I? Before I could speak, Emiko blurted that I was her new boyfriend.

 "Looks like I stumbled into something that isn't my business," I said and tried to walk away. The other two guys grabbed my arms and the third guy, after looking me over, shook his head and they let me go. I put my hands in my pockets and rushed down the street to the corner, where I ducked into a doorway. Emiko and the ex-boyfriend argued. She cried and screamed at him and I heard a slap and then another. I wanted to go help her, but I didn't want three drunken Marines kicking the shit out of me either. I waited in the darkened doorway until I couldn't hear them anymore; and then I waited a while longer. When I finally came out of the doorway and inched into the narrow street, all of them were gone. I hurried to the car, unlocked it and drove towards Gate Two Street. I turned and saw Emiko standing alone a few feet from the corner. She was crying and I called for her to get in the car. I sped on every block back to the apartment, roaring down alleys with the headlights off, trying to insure we were not followed. Emiko kept asking why I had walked away and I lied, saying I'd gone to get help. In the garage beneath the apartment building, she finally stopped sobbing and that's when I saw the rising welt below her left cheek. Upstairs I wrapped ice in a washcloth for her to hold against her face. She explained she had lived with this Marine from Camp Hansen for six months, further explained about the beatings and how one day while he was at work, she left and abandoned all traces of her life when she had been with him. Obviously she hadn't erased all her tracks. For five weeks he had hounded Emiko's friends for information about where she had gone. With his friends he began a systematic search of bars, hotels, anywhere anyone had mentioned she might be found until he had found the two of us together.

The ice did little to reduce the swelling beneath her eye. The flesh was darkening to purple and indigo as she spoke. My only concern was that they might have followed us to the apartment. That's when she said he had told her he was returning to the States the following week. He had been planning to ask her to come with him, but instead told her to go fuck herself, and then he had punched her. I held her until she fell asleep.

When Badger came in that night after a swing shift at Torii Station, he found me sitting in our beanbag chair with a bottle of Akadama wine, Emerson, Lake and Palmer playing on the stereo, and a few candles lit on the crate we used as a coffee table. He sensed right away that something had happened and changed out of his fatigues, joined me, swigging from the wine bottle. I told him about the Marines and he was gung ho to go out and find them. I reminded him that Marines were like wild dogs, they traveled in packs...if we found one, we'd find twenty. That discouraged him a little, so I finally told him if he went out he'd be going out alone. Was he going to challenge every Marine until he found the right one? I said I wanted to be here if Emiko woke up. He surprised me then, telling me to be careful: some people feared not being loved enough, others feared being loved too much. I asked him to elaborate but he clammed up, sat alone reflecting, brooding I thought. He did that at times and there was no force that could shake his concentration.

Emiko woke later and called for me. Badger had gone to bed but I was still listening to music on the living room floor, mulling over just how much of a coward I had been, and numbing my wounded pride with another bottle of wine. I sat down on the bed next to Emiko. Her cheek was severely swollen and she couldn't open her left eye. She wanted to make love, even as she hurt. I suppose she wanted to know she was still wanted, so we made love and she wept during most of it. Have you ever made love to a woman while she cried? It doesn't do much for your sense of self.

I dislike myself for quite a while after that. I felt inadequate for not having done more and I rolled the subject of revenge over in my mind like a ball of clay, imagining the satisfaction I'd glean from breaking the bones in that Marines face. I knew I'd failed a crucial test, not only with Emiko, but with Badger as well. So much of that time is tied up with him. I think what I received from the friendship was a sense of security, as though nothing would harm me when I was in his circle...safe in his shadow. His confidence inspired your own. Had we gone out that night and found Emiko's ex-boyfriend, Badger would have landed the first punch without speaking. He would have fought, would have hurt those men so they would never forget him. He would not have slunk away with his hands in his pockets.

There are times I grow angry with myself, recalling that incident. I have different fears these days, but getting hurt is still one of them. The day we were shot down, Badger and I spent the night in the jungle, suspended by our parachute harnesses in the height of those trees. Fear kept us company, but I had been afraid all day. I didn't tell Badger before we took off, but the briefing about the MiGs had indeed alarmed me. We should not have been flying under those circumstances. There should have been MiGCAP to protect us, as they constantly promised. There were no fighters near us…they scrambled F-4s from Udorn eventually, but the most they were able to do was pinpoint the flaming wreckage of the RC-130 in Laos for the SAR mission. No one's ever where they should be…I was hiding in a doorway when I should have been in that street, punching and getting punched.

Emiko's face stayed black and blue for nearly two weeks. She was sore and wouldn't leave the apartment during that time. She forfeited her job at the record store, most of her friends stopped coming by, and while I was at work she moped around the apartment listening to albums and smoking our dope. One night she argued with Badger about the massing dirty clothes and their odor. He told me about it when I got home. She wouldn't answer my questions about it. I was punishing myself and I didn't need her doing the same. We slept in the same bed, we fucked…even though it seemed more combative than loving…as though we were trying to punish one another with passion. Our communication was entirely physical. There was fondness still, but it was weakening. We had intended the TDY to Cam Ranh, as a vacation from one another, with the intention of working out our problems when I got back. She was gone when I got back to Okinawa.

I can't escape the notion that I was just as cruel to her as if I had beaten her. That night if I had fought, she might have been able to run away, or they might have hurt her even more for my resisting. I don't know…I'll never know. I don't even know if it's important anymore.

5

The day I was discharged, I boarded a bus from Travis Air Force Base to San Francisco International. I debated going straight home to visit my parents, but had been writing to my sister in Denver and she'd invited me to stop over for a while before seeing the folks. I walked into the terminal and one of the guys who got out at the same time asked me to rent a car with him and drive down the coast to Monterey. He pressed pretty strongly, but the idea of seeing the snow-capped Rockies appealed to me more. I approached the first airline counter, booked their next flight to Denver, and then called my sister Trish and relayed my flight information.

Trish is married and has two kids, both girls, and as children we were not overly close. Once we each escaped our parents it seemed we could both talk to one another. She wrote me steadily while I was overseas and somewhere in a basement carton I still have all her letters. A few days ago I took them out and reminisced. I was discharged on Lincoln's birthday and I've always thought that was symbolic. I throw a little party for myself each year to commemorate my emancipation. I've never missed a year.

The day I landed at Stapleton Airport in Denver, I had already shed my uniform and decided I would grow a beard. It was late afternoon and the sun had begun to sink behind the mountains. A smoggy haze had nestled up against the Rockies, shaded orange and purple. It was beautiful and I stood in the tall windows of the terminal and gazed for a few minutes until I felt a hand on my arm. Trish had looped her arm in mine, saying nothing, and joined me in appreciating the sunset. She hadn't brought her children, but her husband, Brad, stood a short distance away. I'd written her about the MiG attack and the crash and she studied me hesitantly, then we hugged with tears coming to our eyes. Brad approached and shook my hand. He's a good man, especially with Trish, who could be headstrong, and he is wonderful with their daughters. He asked for the claim tickets for my luggage, draped a heavy coat over my shoulders…"Didn't think you'd be prepared for the weather," he'd said…then left Trish and me alone.

I'd departed Okinawa little more than forty hours before that moment, at sea level with a temperature near eight-five degrees and a humidity to match. Now I stood a mile high with sub-zero temperatures and the air so dry the wind would chap your lips in a few seconds. My blood was thin and as soon as the three of us walked outside to the parking garage, I shivered violently, even bundled in Brad's coat.

They had a beautiful home and I sat before the fireplace that evening, after the girls were in bed, sipping whiskey and talking with Trish and Brad about their lives. Trish neatly avoided questions about the war or my future. They asked me to stay through the weekend and ride with them to their cabin near Evergreen. They rented it to a woman each winter and the furnace was acting up. A local repairman had been contacted but Brad, who was a bit of a control freak, wanted to check out the situation. I agreed and on Saturday, wedged between Kathleen and Margaret in the backseat of the family van, we traveled up the interstate toward Evergreen. In town we stopped and I bought each of the girls a small, carved wooden antelope. The road to the cabin was a twisting gravel channel between three-foot-high snow banks left by the plows. With a stone chimney, the cabin itself stood one story. Smoke filtered into the clear air. The woman who rented it, a sculptor, had converted half of the horse barn into a studio. Brad greeted her as we got out of the car and then went to check on the furnace. Trish watched the girls climb the icy slope toward the ridgeline. When they tired we retreated to the cabin and sat around a ball-and-claw footed table. The sculptor made hot cocoa for the girls and coffee for us. She poured brandy in our mugs. The cabin had three rooms: the kitchen, a single bedroom, and the dining-living room combination. Before the fireplace there was a small, sunken area, filled with pillows. It was a cozy place and I remember wishing I could simply hole up there for the rest of the winter like some misanthropic hermit.

Trish and I went for a walk along the road. The girls reclined on the pillows before the fireplace with their hot chocolate. On either side of the road sat boulders, some taller than the cabin. The sky shone brilliant blue and lofty clouds folded in on one another, their outlines slowly but constantly morphing. We played the child's game of telling each other what we visualized in the cloud shapes. It was easy to talk with Trish, but I couldn't tell her much beyond the brief accounts I'd written in letters to her. I don't think she would have understood and I didn't want to burden her with the responsibility of knowing about it. While we were watching a hawk circling above the tree line, Brad honked the van's horn. On the walk back to the cabin, I stopped to gather rocks, small ones and then larger ones, constructing a pyramid a little less than a foot high at the north side of a huge boulder that bordered the road. Was I thinking about the day Badger died? Probably. Are those stones still piled beside that boulder? Probably not. I've been to Denver twice since that visit but Brad and Trish long ago sold the cabin and bought a condominium near Vail. The sculptor, Trish wrote, died years ago.

In Koza, in Okinawa, an old man managed a taco shop. Charlie's Tacos was famous and after a night of drinking, stopping there was nearly obligatory. He fried the tortillas in front of you and his wife and daughters cooked the meat, shredded the lettuce and cheese, and chopped the tomatoes. Whenever we'd go in, Badger would order three horse tacos. He was certain Charlie couldn't sell them so cheaply if they were made with beef. Charlie set the tacos in a cardboard box lined with tin foil and Badger would whinny every time he bit into one. Good eating when you'd filled your belly with beer. We'd stop there twice a week and when we returned from a TDY to Cam Ranh, Badger's first meal was half a dozen Charlie's tacos. We'd drop off our laundry with the mamasan at the barracks, change into some clean clothes, and then catch a taxi to Gate Two and walk through the crowded streets to Charlie's hole in the wall. It was a small storefront and not a well-kept secret. There couldn't have been more than four tiny tables in the place and if you were fortunate enough to get one, you ended up with someone's elbow in your food half the time.

One night Badger and I took some speed, diet pills were easily attainable from Okinawan pharmacists, and were methodically working our way down one side of BC Street, stopping at each bar for one beer. It was a variation of a game we'd played in language school in El Paso. A group of us would gather in the barracks and write the names of Juarez bars on individual slips of paper. Once across the border in Mexico, we'd pull the slips out one by one, find the bar, down a beer, pull out another slip, and repeat…repeat…repeat. Whoever endured to the final bar was declared winner. The losers chipped in to buy him a whore to cap the evening. But this night Badger and I went door-to-door down BC Street, buzzing nicely, the beer getting us drunk, the speed preventing us from passing out and giving us hope that we could canvas every bar. Late in the evening Badger veered off onto a side street and headed straight to Charlie's. He wolfed down three tacos, grinned at Charlie, walked outside and puked into a binjo ditch.

I helped him to a steam bath and he sang through the entire experience. It was well into the morning and the girls treated it like a party. I gave them money for beer and before long Badger and I were seated, naked, in a humid room with four or five Okinawan girls dancing with one another to Japanese pop music. Beer bottles lined the window sills and an old mamasan sat in a chair in the corner, clapping her hands together and flashing a grin with far too few teeth in it.

Badger reveled in pleasure so he created it around himself. No dull life for him. A boyish spark always ignited his eyes. Magical times. He preferred the non-A sign bars in Koza. The American military concocted a system for approving bars for Americans to patronize. An establishment would be inspected, like a health department inspection, to see if a bar met certain standards. The inspector gave a thumbs-up or a thumbs-down and if the bar won approval, it was able to display a gaudy red capital A near the front door. If it failed, then no red A. We were all warned never to enter a non-A sign bar, but never told why. It could have been as simple as not having separate toilets for men and women. Badger and I soon discovered that the most comfortable bars on the island didn't have A signs. The bar to which I took Emiko when her ex-boyfriend found us was a non-A sign bar.

We became regulars at one or two non-A sign bars, getting to know the bartenders. I celebrated my twenty-second birthday in a non-A sign bar. Badger had arranged a surprise party…food, plum wine, sake, and an Australian stripper, who we learned usually worked officers' clubs throughout Japan. She must have been nearing forty by then, and she was beautiful. She danced with a six-foot boa constrictor. She carried her pet around in a cloth shopping bag and wore a long coat from club to club. If you didn't know she was a stripper, you'd probably think she was just another woman on her way home, except of course for the white skin and blonde hair. She performed for us that night and the things she did with that snake…I expected it to suffocate.

Badger claimed to have slept with her but I doubted that. He worshipped Asian women, said they were the most beautiful women in the world, even toyed with coming back to Asia after his discharge. He wanted to visit Thailand; he said he'd heard that the most beautiful women on earth lived in a northwest town of Thailand called Chiang Mai. It was just one of those things a guy says. But I doubt he would have lived in the jungle…he always loved the ocean. Given a choice, Badger would have preferred an island and its beaches. That's why he liked Cam Ranh. There's no coastline in Laos…it's landlocked.

I'm amazed sometimes at what triggers memory. The other night in the bar a group of students ordered shots of tequila, slurping them with lime and salt. It reminded me of a night in Juarez when a group of us spent an extremely cheap evening at a Mexican bar (if it had been in Koza, it would have been a non-A sign bar), where tequila shots sold for a dime apiece. We were always short of money and this was one of those end-of-the-month drunks. The first time we wandered into that bar, we felt like intruders among the old regulars. The prices were right and we were persistent, so eventually the bartender came to expect us toward the end of each month. He was thin-faced man with shoulder-length hair that he greased straight back from his forehead. He always wore a white shirt with no pockets and a skinny black tie. Whenever we came in he greeted us with a laugh and would clear out the corner booth for us.

This night we staged a drinking contest, a "shots" contest. One shot of tequila each, round after round, until there was a last man standing. The bartender sold us a bottle and set out eight shot glasses, and then he frowned and walked back behind the bar. The first shots went down easily...one or two coughs and some deep heaves. Badger, sitting nearest the bar in the booth, watched with his usual passivity. He could piss me off when he'd flutter on the periphery of something, behaving as though the entire affair was beneath him. Lofty yes, but not too lofty to watch.

The shot glasses were refilled, and one by one, downed again. We'd heard stories of men who had drunk a bottle of tequila, stood up, and then keeled over with heart failure. So we amended the contest rules that no one could drink more than one shot every fifteen minutes. I mean, we wanted to be careful. No one had planned for this drinkfest, so not everyone had eaten before we crossed the bridge to Juarez. Badger bought bags of pretzels and chips and passed them around. By the time my third shot had been poured and I was holding it in my hand, my head was fuzzy and there was salt on my fingers from probing the bag of potato chips. I sipped from the glass at first, then quickly tipped it back and let the tequila burn my throat. By then it could have been diesel fuel for all I knew...I had lost the ability to taste it. I could only feel it searing my mouth and gums. One of the other guys was munching on the Cheetos Badger had set before him. A cheer and applause erupted when everyone finished their shots. Some of the other customers had begun to watch what we were doing, and a few of the old men in the bar took bets on who would win and who would be the first to drop out. Springer was there and he got some action...bets that he wouldn't finish the contest. He looked woozy and was cradling his chin on the palm of his hand, but it teetered back and forth as his arm swayed, his elbow precariously perched on the tabletop. Badger had turned away and was watching a show on the TV. I was pissed at him now.

The fourth and fifth shots went down, but on the seventh, Springer choked and pushed what was left in his glass across the table, muttering that he'd had enough. He struggled to his feet and stumbled to the bathroom door, saying he was going to piss his pants any minute. The gathered crowd laughed, some pesos exchanged hands and one of the old men refilled the glasses. The fifteen minute rule was abandoned as we reached for the glasses and drained them. One guy…I've tried to remember his name, but can't – I know he was from Ohio, that's all…shivered violently when he placed his glass on the table, then warded off the Mexican's hand when he tried to refill it from the bottle. I was more than affected by the booze at this point, watching myself with some detachment reach for the bag of potato chips again, trying to find a position in which my feet felt comfortable on the floor. Springer returned, paler than before, and we all recognized that he hadn't merely pissed. Badger regarded him as he sat down, then went to the bar and retrieved a glass of ice water and a cold towel. Springer looked ill and I should have realized what that meant for the rest of us if we continued. The crowd encouraged us to drink and we downed our shots, some very slowly. Another bottle was delivered to the table and the glasses refilled. One of the old men passed some bills to the bartender, who frowned but said nothing.

Tony Ashton watched the old man who had filled the glasses grin and motion for him to drink again; Ashton returned a wide-mouthed smile, lifted his glass to his mouth. Badger told Tony to take his time, that these buzzards weren't going anywhere. I looked at him but didn't smile; I was beyond drunk at that point and hated Badger's indifference. Tony gagged then and lurched to his feet, swinging towards the bathroom. As he did he vomited in an arc, like a creepy painter he sprayed the canvas of old Mexicans who had gathered around the table. Pandemonium. The bartender screamed at the old woman who cleaned the place, then rounded the bar and hurried her to the area with a mop and bucket. The water smelled no better than Ashton's vomit. Badger stood and walked to the far end of the bar and sat on a stool. As they wiped their shirts and pants with bar rags, the old Mexicans laughed and clapped one another on their backs. The bartender was furious and cursed loudly as he supervised the clean-up. When Tony emerged from the bathroom, the crowd cheered and some of the men collected their winnings. Tony hadn't gotten a single drop of puke on himself, but he had lacquered a dozen others. We all shuffled out of the bar and when the air hit me, I rushed down an alley and puked as well. Badger waited on the street and I got pissed at him for that, too. I didn't understand why he acted like that at times. He rarely drank much…called it a lifer's hobby…but he'd always come along and nurse a beer while the rest of us blitzed ourselves into numbness. I suppose he felt he represented the voice of reason.

On that last flight, about an hour into the mission, his mood changed to that air of detachment he could adopt. His moods taught me patience, which had always been in short supply. We sat at our positions but neither of us had any traffic up. I was killing time talking, not through the intercom but with one side of my headset slipped off. I was leaning toward him, speaking loudly over the engine noise and maybe that's what set him off. He listened for a while without watching me, then turned abruptly and told me to shut the fuck up. Did I have to run my mouth all the time? Even with close friends that happens, so I didn't think much of it at the time. I put my headset back on and twirled my tuning knob, searching through the frequencies. I looked at him later and he sat staring at his receivers, in his mood.

Did he have a premonition? Who the hell knows. He'd get like that...clam up and hide in himself...it was a way of finding solitude. An hour and a half later, he snapped out of it, went back to the galley and fixed lunch. I joined him and we talked as though nothing had happened. It was chillier near the aircraft's tail and one thing we had learned was that if you lay down on the loading ramp, the engines' vibrations gave you a fantastic back massage. After a few hours at our intercept positions, our necks and shoulders would stiffen and ache. Badger began detailing for me the stereo system he was going to buy when he got back to Okinawa. He'd saved nearly a thousand dollars and had picked out all the components. He only needed to buy them, crate them and ship them home. He was going to live in San Francisco. We'd spent a few days together before we left Travis for Okinawa and he became infatuated with the city. He'd grown up in Indiana and had never been to a major league baseball game until we went to Candlestick Park and watched the Giants lose to the Mets. He talked about settling in San Francisco, where he could continue to watch the sun set over the Pacific. His ultimate goal of returning to the Far East seemed more attainable if he was already sitting on the west coast, than if he was stranded in Terre Haute.

We never considered staying together after we were discharged. Badger said I could come visit him in San Francisco and I suppose that said as much about what he wanted when we got out as much as anything could. There seemed a tacit agreement that after we walked out of the gates of Travis, we might need some time away from one another. Would we be still be close today? Or was our friendship situational? Did the Air Force manufacture our friendship, banding us together in opposition to a common enemy? I hadn't decided what I was going to do after I got out. Memphis had been the only home I'd known, and I thought I might visit some friends there, see some old places. The familiarity of the city was attractive, after all the newness that had been thrust at me during the past three years. There's always stability and security in the known. I wasn't as certain as Badger seemed about San Francisco. He said he would live on a street that overlooked the ocean with a view of the Golden Gate Bridge. There's a story that the Golden Gate is constantly being painted, that when the painting crew completes its trek from one end to the other, the paint has worn down at the starting point and they have to begin again. The war was a lot like that bridge.

Lindsay took a day off yesterday and we drove up to Mount Simon Park on Dell's Pond. We hadn't done that in a few years. I've often fantasized what my return from overseas would have been like if I'd been married to Lindsay at the time. She lived in Omaha, Nebraska then. The day would have been cold and snowy and Eppley Airfield would have been layered in exhaust haze. I shiver as the airplane glides over Council Bluffs and I see the streets, dark strips, intersecting in a lattice of white snow cover. I have journeyed from the tropical warmth of the Pacific to the dreadful cold of the Great Plains. To every emotion, for every movement, there is a balance. It's fitting that I fly home and it's appropriate that I'm alone after being surrounded by friends for the past four years. The aircraft lands with a roar. We taxi to the terminal. People ignore the flight attendants and stand to retrieve items from the overhead storage bins before the plan comes to a stop, discussing mundane subjects like the weather. But this weather isn't mundane to me...I haven't seen snow in three years. In the year we spent in El Paso, we counted three days of precipitation, and that included one morning when at three o'clock someone ran through the barracks hallway screaming "It's snowing!" Dozens of us poured outside in our underwear, gawking at the snow floating down. We crafted dwarf snowmen, lobbed snowballs at one another, and then watched it melt as the sun stretched across the base from the desert to our east. Every trace of it had disappeared by noon... even our meager snowmen.

The sight of snow as I inch down the aisle is welcome. It's chilly in the jet way and as I stride up the incline toward the terminal I hear voices. In this fantasy I'm in uniform, and as I emerge into the waiting area, Lindsay sees me and begins to cry as I push the crowd to reach her and hold her tightly in my arms. We clutch one another for a long time and then I'm crying...feeling exceptionally happy. There's so much relief at being home with Lindsay, I suppose because the actual homecoming in Memphis was far less dramatic.

My father met me at the airport, saying Mom didn't want to face the traffic. He insisted we go an airport lounge and get a drink, when all I wanted to do was collect my luggage and get out of there. How could I explain to him my aversion to airports and aircraft? I've rarely flown in the years since...mostly for funerals. Eventually we put my bags in the back of his station wagon and headed home. Dad wanted to show me some of the changes in the town since I'd left. The high school had a new gym...I stopped him mid-sentence. "I just want to go home," I told him. "I'm tired." He relented. While I had been in the service, the house I'd grown up in had been demolished to make way for expansion of Memphis State University. My parents now lived in a new house south of Park Avenue where all the streets were named after locations and characters from Robin Hood. As Dad pulled into the driveway of a home I'd never seen before, I felt all connection with my past evaporate. It was all gone. I called old friends and spoke with many of their parents…many had left Memphis: for school, for the war, or simply to be someplace else. We strove, many of us, to separate ourselves, to claim independence. I don't think that's such an important goal these days.

When Dad finally got me home, I felt that perhaps I had cheated him, remembering that whenever he'd wanted to talk to me, he'd suggest we go for a drive. That's when we'd talk, when he'd mull things over with me. I wondered if he and Mom talked the way the two of us did during those drives. They were married for more than forty years when he died, and I don't remember the two of them talking when my brothers and sisters and I were around them. Whenever Mom calls, Lindsay usually talks with her longer than I do. I wonder if it's possible to die of boredom…if so, that's what did in my father. That day when he pulled the station wagon into the driveway, he honked the horn three times, his eternal signal that he was home. The entire neighborhood knew when Bob Hunter got home. If we kids were playing down the street, we always knew when to come home for supper. We'd leave when we heard the horn. That day Mom stood by the living room picture window, staring while Dad muscled my bags from the car, refusing my help. "Go see your Mom," he said. "She's waited a long time…and be sure to give her a kiss." I walked in to the house and was shocked to see how much smaller she seemed. I towered over her. Her hair looked coarser but not gray…I assumed she colored it. The creases around her eyes had deepened and the skin on her hands seemed tightly drawn. I'd never thought of her as an old woman. She was teary-eyed and reached her arms out to me, expecting me to cross the room and embrace her. That was my homecoming and it wasn't what I was expecting. That night there was a small get-together of friends and family. Not my close friends, my parents' close friends. That's when it began to occur to me that I would not be staying long. Not just for the party, but in Memphis. I had nothing to say to those people, no common experience any more. I believed I had changed dramatically during the past four years and they hadn't changed at all.

For the first week or two I was the prized houseguest, but then some familiar patterns began to reassert themselves. As the novelty of the solider-son wore off, I began to become Bob and Betty's little boy again. They began asking where I was going each night and when I'd be home. I bristled, wondering how they could expect my life to resume where it'd left off four years earlier. Could they not understand that while they may be the same people they had been, I certainly wasn't? Had they grown a blind spot to my growth? I knew they'd worried about me. Dad had written that Mom had nearly had a breakdown when she learned of the crash. Even the news that I was fine and had been removed from flight status hadn't seemed to calm her, he'd said. They ignored the subject, never asked me to talk about what had happened. The kind of avoidance that makes it obvious that you either don't want to talk about it or don't know how to bring it up. I would have sat down with them, but they never gave me any indication they wanted to hear about it. My Dad served in the Marines in World War II, island-hopping through the Pacific, and I expected he would have understood how at times I just wanted to scream, to be out of control long enough to let some of the anger escape, to vent that inner rage. Our wars were so different.

In the fictional reunion with Lindsay, with the tears and long hugs at the airport, we'd get in her car and ride home. There'd be no party and no banner like the one my father draped across the mantle welcoming me back. That was terrible. It would be just Lindsay and me, sitting over dinner, enjoying the sensation that the entire ordeal had been worth it because I'd come home to her, to a woman who had loved and missed me, who had gone to sleep each night worried about me. Considering how I had whored and drunk my way through so much of my time away, it's easy to believe that you receive the homecoming you deserve. Back to my Catholic roots: your suffering will be rewarded, my son. Always the quid pro quo on the sacrifice and reward bullshit. It amazes me that people still bow down to that crap…they're just another breed of lifers. Mom and Dad were upset when I told them I was leaving, but the conformity they shoved at me was intolerable. The trappings of their life turned my stomach and I knew that if I had stayed, one day they were going to push me a little too far and I'd push back in an ugly scene. I wanted to be left alone, but that didn't seem obvious to my parents. They wanted to fit me into a comfortable shoe…no aberrations.

6

A friend of mine died this past week. Nobody from the war; a friend from the university. He rolled his car off a ramp on the interstate and both he and his wife died. Jim and I were history majors. After graduation he went into sales at a pharmaceutical company. We'd kept in loose touch since we left school, the four of us getting together for dinner or for drinks every few weeks. He was a good, if not close, friend. There are guys you sit down with, drink a few beers, spill some of your soul. It wasn't like that with Jim. There had been a few late night sessions during college, fewer since then. Over cards our conversations wouldn't delve any deeper than what I'd have with a stranger at the bar. Then again, some folks are more apt to be candid with a stranger than with someone they know. There are less risks being honest with a stranger.

I don't mean I was dishonest with Jim. We never approached any level where candor would have made any difference. Jim had avoided the war and the two of us met at a time when the war still occupied most of my consciousness. Lindsay and I went to the funeral, his family is all from around Eau Claire, and they thanked us at the cemetery for coming. They were hurting and I felt genuine empathy for them. When I got out of the Air Force, I believed I would never again grieve for anyone. I waited for someone close to me to die, to test myself, to see if I could cry for someone. Thankfully I haven't faced that test.

There was a bar in Juarez called the Cave, and it's the only place where I ever saw Badger truly stinking drunk. The Cave's most unique feature was its entertainment. One of the guys in our squadron who had gone there told us we shouldn't miss the show, but wouldn't tell us anything more. One Saturday night Badger and I threaded our way to this place. It was tucked away, far from the main streets. There was no sign outside, just some guy out front, who took our cover charge and pushed us through a door. We entered a long, low-ceilinged corridor, the walls roughly plastered and painted various shades of gray. Cave walls, I suppose. We emerged into a small, hot room that reeked of stale beer. I noticed there were no tables, just chairs lining the walls. Stalactites and stalagmites molded from the same ashy plaster as the corridor had been mounted on the floor and the ceiling; they had over time begun to crumble into gummy piles on the floor. In the middle of the floor lay cushions. I followed Badger to the bar and ordered a beer; he ordered brandy, but the bartender laughed and said she'd bring him a tequila. When she returned with our drinks, Badger asked her name. "Rosa," she said. Dark-haired, dark-eyed, older than she seemed in the dim bar, but pretty enough. Badger and I had been drinking for some time before we made it to the Cave, and he was showing the effects. I can't for the life of me remember why he was drinking; it was, as I've said, totally unlike him to get drunk, to risk losing control. Badger hummed along with the country music on the jukebox and signaled Rosa for a refill. "You're pretty," he told her, slurring his words a bit when she filled his glass. She measured him up and said she didn't think he could do anything about that tonight. Badger said he'd appreciate an opportunity. Rosa laughed and moved down the bar; Badger watched her as he slammed the shot of tequila and beckoned her back with the bottle. She smiled and asked Badger if he really, really wanted her. He nodded as the lights in the bar dimmed and a single spot illuminated the cushions in the center of the room. When I looked back at the bar, Rosa was gone and the guy from the front door had unplugged the jukebox in mid-song. Several guys whistled and then the scratchy sound of a phonograph needle gave way to slow, loud music. Rosa, wearing nothing but her underwear, slunk into the lighted circle, writhing and twisting until the end of the song. She removed her bra, threw it behind the bar, and then pranced around the edge of the crowd as another song started. In just her panties she danced until the end of the second song, then stripped them off. The spotlight narrowed and grew slightly dimmer; the music grew louder. Now totally naked, Rosa slowly moved through the crowd of cheering, sweating men until she stopped in front of Badger and crooked her finger at him. Suddenly two men grabbed Badger and dragged him into the center of the circle. They flung him on the cushions as Rosa straddled him, bouncing on his stomach. She crept forward until her pussy was directly over his face. Everyone was hooting. Then the two guys unbuckled Badger's belt and ripped his jeans and underwear off him. Catcalls from the audience. Rosa kneeled beside him and started to lick his cock. Badger reached out to grab one of her breasts but she expertly slapped his hand away. She bent over, whispered something to him; he smiled, nodded and laced his hands behind his head. He laid there, content and happy as the drunk fool he was. This was the show we'd been promised.

Rosa gripped his cock, flopping it back and forth against Badger's thighs. Cheers, shouting, clapping. I didn't think there was any way she was going to get him hard, but she knelt beside him and started to suck him, gripping most of him in her hand so that she only licked the head. The crowd went wild. Rosa's head was bobbing wildly, but most of it was exaggeration for the show, although I'm sure there were some guys there who believed she was gorging herself on Badger's cock. Then she stood and lowered herself on Badger's face, grinding her pussy on his nose. She moaned dramatically and the crowd screamed for her to suffocate him. The two guys returned as Rosa stood. They turned Badger onto his hands and knees as Rosa shimmied beneath him and locked her legs around the back of his knees. He collapsed on her as she started moaning loud encouragements: "Come on big boy! Fuck me!" Badger was pumping and the crowd was chanting with each down stroke, like cheerleaders. Then the two guys began passing out bar straws, one by one to every guy in the bar. One guy reached out and stuck his straw in the crack of Badger's ass. He swatted at it, but missed. Another guy reached forward and tried to butt-fuck Badger with a straw. Badger managed to swat away some of the straws, but there were always a few in his butt crack. Rosa's legs were sinuous and when Badger tried to twist himself to slap at the straws, she locked him tightly. Ten minutes elapsed when Rosa began to pound her hands on Badger's back and scream, faking her orgasm for the crowd. I don't think Badger was even in her. The two guys lifted Badger off Rosa and as he sat back I could see his cock was indeed soft. She stood, wet her fingers in her pussy and then wiped them on Badger's upper lip. Rosa then skipped into the back room as Badger grinned like an imbecile. The spotlight dimmed as the house lights came back on, and the jukebox came back to life with the same country song. Badger sat in the middle of the room, surrounded by straws, his pants still around his ankles, touching his finger to his lip and smelling it. I got him to his feet, helped him pull up his jeans, and then the two of us ambled to the bar, where Rosa stood, clothed again, holding the tequila bottle out to Badger.

    On the way back to base, I forced Badger to eat some sandwiches, then held his head while he vomited in the gutter and made him shut up when we walked past a pair of Juarez policemen when he wanted to ask them if they knew Rosa. At the bridge on the border with El Paso, I coached him so he would state he was a citizen of the U.S. and had nothing to declare when questioned by the customs agents. Drunks who thought they were being funny by declaring themselves Norwegian citizens were sometimes locked up for a few hours to teach them a lesson. But he was so drunk then he simply answered the questions when prompted and we reentered the U.S. with no trouble.

I never saw him that wasted again. He was sick the following day, but not as sick as I thought he deserved to be.

We didn't drink and whore all the time. In Okinawa, Badger and I often went snorkeling. The water was clear as the sky and the reefs offered spectacular scenery. We'd borrow a car and drive north toward Nago. One spot I remember formed a natural amphitheater…a beach with bright red sand surrounded by squat shrub trees on the slopes of a rocky hollow. A hundred yards offshore sat a reef where we'd snorkel. Okinawa wore a myriad of colors: the blue of the water and sky, green on the hills, blacks and browns in the rocks, and the orange and red of the coral. Not to mention the fish. Such colors as they paused in front of us or darted away in a shimmer, and such a relief from the drab blue, silver and green of military life.

One day we floated on the surface beyond the reef in water that was about ten or twelve feet deep, after having smoked some dope to keep me from feeling too anxious about how far from the shore we had ventured. I'm not a great swimmer, and while the flippers gave me confidence, the dope mellowed me out enough that I would accompany Badger out that far. Badger dove for a moment to pursue a baby octopus, trailing it for a few yards. I floated, gazing straight down at the coral below me, reveling in the warmth of the ocean. Suddenly the water temperature grew colder and below me a shaft appeared, about ten feet across, like a dark and bottomless tunnel. It so startled me in my state that I immediately reared back and tried to stand up in the water, so overcome was I with the sensation of falling into that hole, as though it was sucking me down into it. The mouthpiece of my snorkel fell from between my teeth in my panic and I gasped a mouthful of water. I pitched my head above the surface and yelled for Badger. He couldn't hear me…he was still underwater. I felt stupid then, but the sensation of skimming the surface of shallow water and then encountering that never-ending shaft frightened the hell out of me. I splashed on the surface for a moment or two then settled down and replaced my mouthpiece. I stayed closer to the shore after that, in water in which I could stand.

We did a lot of things like that; we weren't always in bars. Some afternoons we'd sit on the roof of our apartment when we weren't on duty and simply talk through a long afternoon. We'd discuss the war, speculating about when it would end. We both agreed the end would be a political and not a military decision. Had the combat been governed by military decisions, the Army would have been occupying Hanoi by then. But Nixon had his hands on the controls, the Paris peace talks held the front page headlines, and our flights over Laos allowed us to monitor battle results. Badger believed war was an American disease and although the Vietnamese war might end, those of us not devoured by the disease would become carriers, and at some point in the future we'd launch another war; it would erupt like a boil. We'd never be rid of war. Conversations with Badger were always provocative, if not comfortable. One guy in our squadron, on one of those do-nothing days at our apartment, approached Badger for his help in starting an underground newspaper. Badger listened to him list his issues: work schedules, living conditions. The guy had never been to Cam Ranh and slept on a lice-infested mattress, but he wanted to complain about the air-conditioned, maid-cleaned barracks on Okinawa. Badger stopped his ramblings at one point and asked him what he was going to say in his newspaper about the war. The guy balked. Badger rose and headed toward the stairway from the building's roof. "Listen, asshole," he told him. "Gore the bull or don't attack the herd."

I don't know where he came up with things like that. He was intelligent, no doubt, and his hate for the war was unquestioned. But he was also capable of separating his own role in it from his principles. Not once did he hesitate to board the aircraft, sit at his intercept position, and perform the tasks that were his "duty." He never stopped being an accessory to something he professed to oppose.

On the day of that final mission, when we took off from Cam Ranh, the sunrise was beautiful. Gold and silver sparking over the bay, shadows creeping along the revetment walls. I wondered if Badger flew to get away from the war, creating distance from it by sequestering himself in the aircraft, striving for that separation even as he listened to it. Like going to a movie wearing a blindfold. There's no question he wanted to be rid of the war, no doubt at all. This is all jumbled in my memory. There was one focal point on that last flight to distinguish it from all the others. The entire morning seemed out of sync, like when the soundtrack doesn't match up with the picture in that same movie. There's no simple way to say it, but from the moment Badger woke me that morning, there was an otherness to the day. I felt outside myself at times, almost drugged, so that at the same moment I was aware of what was happening around me but incapable of doing anything except following my same routine, like a wind-up doll. I have wondered if this is revisionist history or if I indeed felt that way, helpless to deviate from what I'd always done. Like a twig in the gutter after a storm, being carried along. Badger was distant; I was off-center and wary of the MiG report. I was nervous about flying, as though I'd been doing it long enough to be tempting the law of averages. There had never been an attack on an RC-130 or RC-135 during the war until that day. From one point of view that was a record just begging to be broken. On one flight out of Kadena a few months earlier, the copilot had rushed back to the window near my position and plugged his headset into my intercom panel. He looked out and examined the engines and then told the pilot we were losing fuel like a son-of-a-bitch. He signaled me to removed my headset and cautioned me not to repeat what I'd heard. I nodded, but when he returned to the cockpit, I strapped myself into my parachute harness. People noticed and a chain reaction began; they all knew I listened to MiGs, and when they saw me strapping in they assumed the worst: that we were being attacked. As word spread, everyone stopped working and began preparing to bail out. The AMS got pissed. The pilot, when he found out what was happening in his back end, got pissed. We diverted to Clark AFB in the Philippines and landed safely. They repaired the fuel leak and we returned to Kadena. That flight marked the beginning of my uneasiness with flying. Even now I hesitate to fly. The sense of helplessness overcomes me each time. That afternoon when the missiles hit the right wing of the RC-130 and opened the side of the aircraft like a can opener, I had been listening to those pilots from when they took off from Phuc Yen to the moment when they fired their rockets and laughed doing so.

    Our MiGCAP wasn't anywhere near where it was supposed to be. Some of us speculated we had been dangled out there as bait for the MiGs to strike. A sacrifice to justify massive retaliatory raids against their airfields. Were we a worm on a hook? Exchange one unarmed aircraft and its crew for the right to carpet-bomb Hanoi. I hope if that is the truth that I never find out. I would kill those responsible, even now.

From the moment we got on orbit and started searching for radio traffic we sensed something was odd. There was no traffic up, not any of the customary frequencies, none of the usual chatter we could count on to break up the monotony. Like the old war movie cliché: it was too quite out there. Badger didn't hear any SAM traffic for two hours and aside from the two MiGs who came up after us, there were no other aircraft flying in North Vietnam that day. I didn't hear a single damned aircraft. Even ground communications were sparse.

For lunch we ate boned turkey that we heated in the oven, and spooned it out over wheat bread. Apple juice. Springer loved the stuff. He was one of the last to exit the bird and he landed about five miles from Badger and me, in a clearing. Some villagers spotted him so he ran toward a tree line and was picked up by a Jolly Green out of Nakhon Phanom with an hour. We were close to the Thai border when we were hit and the pilot did what he could to head the plane west before the crew bailed out. Badger and I dropped near the village of Lak Sao, in the vicinity of a North Vietnamese base camp…that's why there were so many unfriendlies around. We plummeted into pretty thick jungle and our parachute lines got tangled in tall trees. We could see one another but didn't dare speak, and I never even considered lowering myself to the ground. Each parachute contained about two-hundred feet of nylon rope, and if you chose, you could lower yourself from a tree perch. But we heard voices below us within minutes of crashing through the tree limbs. Altitude was safety.

I still wonder if when I remember this I embellish. Was there really something different about that day? Maybe I'm compensating and imagining I should have felt something different. We used to joke that missions out of Cam Ranh were a cinch, because the mission was ten hours shorter than a Kadena-based flight. Anyone could handle a mission out of Cam Ranh standing on his head...or maybe even hanging from a tree, huh? It's not fun hanging in a parachute harness for any extended period of time, especially not overnight in the jungle when people on the ground are trying to find you and kill you. I glanced at Badger in the seconds before we bailed out and his expression was fascinating...he stood by the loading ramp and looked back at the hole in the fuselage. You could see the ground through the jagged opening. I had yelled at him as we fought against the wind and crept out of our compartment. We had put on our helmets and parachutes before the missiles hit, and one by one we dove out the open ramp from fifteen- or sixteen-thousand feet. I saw three men falling below me and looked up to find Badger. I saw the aircraft begin to spin...a good portion of the right wing was blown away except for the tip and a thread section of the leading edge. I spread my arms and legs and free fell as we had been trained to do until my parachute deployed automatically. I twisted around and was surprised to see Badger so close to me as we fell into the trees.

There was a time when I felt my marriage was hemming me in and I'd imagine being single again. Preoccupation with the past is an old man's hobby. When I imagined being single, I lived where I live now, worked where I work now, but Lindsay wasn't with me. It's not that we were divorced, I fantasized that she died, usually in a car wreck or something else appropriately tragic. I sat alone and quiet in my living room, after the funeral, drinking a whiskey. I don't indulge that fantasy any more. There are times with Lindsay when we're in bed together, just before we go to sleep, when I look at her and feel as though she's someone I've never known. If she catches me staring at her, she'll smile and say "What?" I'll laugh and tell her I'm having one of those moments when I realize I'll never leave her because she's still an unsolved mystery…the woman I've loved all these years still has undiscovered recesses.

Early on in our marriage, when I worked afternoons in the bar, a woman walked in; I had slept with her a few times before meeting Lindsay. She wanted to go out after I got off. I called Lindsay and said I'd be late, that I was going to hang with a guy I knew. "Have a good time," she'd said, but I heard the hesitation and suspicion in her voice. The woman and I fooled around at her place until almost midnight, and I had gotten off work at four-thirty. Even as I rose to go home, she urged me stay. Before I dressed, I wet a washcloth in the bathroom and tried to scrub the smell from me.

Lindsay was in bed and I knew there'd be tension; it wasn't the first time I'd pulled that number on her. In the bathroom I brushed my teeth and tried again to wash the women's scent off me. I would have showered, but I never shower at night and it seemed like that would be as good as a confession to Lindsay. I slipped into bed, hoping Lindsay might feign sleep to avoid a confrontation. But she asked if I was drunk. I admitted I was probably a little drunk and she asked where we'd gone. I named a few bars and leaned over to kiss her, but she turned her cheek in a sly move. She was twisted at an awkward angle with her back to me, peering over shoulder. It must have been uncomfortable, so turning away as I leaned in to kiss her seemed perfectly natural. Offering me her cheek left me wondering if she was angry or simply trying to avoid a neck cramp. If she was trying to make me feel guilty, she succeeded. Of course, I may have been trying to make myself feel guilty for cheating on her, for hurting her. Back then when I fantasized about being alone, I suppose it rose from not feeling totally content with Lindsay, as though she was inadequate in some manner. One time after a serious argument, I imagined the death scenario again. The difference that time was that instead of a tragic accident, this time I killed Lindsay and passed it off as an accident. In the house we rented then, the stairway was uncarpeted wood and often slippery for stocking feet. Lindsay had been drinking, no doubt fueling our argument. I imagined lying in bed beside her, waiting for her to fall asleep. Then I reach around, wedge her neck in the crook of an elbow, place my free hand at the back of her head and snap forward, breaking her neck. I drag her body to the top of the stairs, prop her upright and then pitch her down the stairs. Everyone believes she broke her neck in the fall. Regrettable. The funeral has all the pomp it deserves and I find myself again sitting at home alone and quiet, with my whiskey.

 Guilt was how I felt that night with Lindsay. She didn't ask me any more questions so I didn't have to manufacture any more lies. The next morning she didn't say much, just went to work. The heaviest guilt came with my hangover. The woman and I had gotten really drunk before we did anything. It often happened that way: I needed the numbing before I could ignore my conscience, but the following morning brought hangover punishment and the guilt. I would imagine that Lindsay knew everything, that she had smelled the woman on me and had chosen to suffer quietly. I'd drive myself to the verge of crying, of wanting to call her, confess and beg her forgiveness. But I never said anything. I acted normally while she went about her routines in a manner that I took as either boredom or reservation. I was left hanging, not knowing what to do about the guilt. I've inflicted a lot of pain on her, some intentional and some unintentional. We know a great deal about one another's weaknesses and we have learned to rely on one another's strengths.

Every morning after I cheated on Lindsay, I'd tell myself it was the last time. For a long time in my life I believed there would never be a last time, there was only a next time.

After the crash, when I returned to Kadena, there were extensive debriefings. The incident garnered national press attention. I had listened to the two MiGs so I was included in nearly every phase of the investigation. It was exhausting. I had wrenched muscles in my back when I landed in the trees and was wearing a brace for a few weeks, as well as enjoying a numbing dose of Valium. After a few weeks the report was issued: human error was eliminated…everyone was exonerated. It had been a devastating but unavoidable incident of war. Phuc Yen airfield was bombed in retaliation. I was given two weeks recuperation leave. I traveled to Japan and Hong Kong, drinking every night. Back at Kadena the flight surgeon examined me and certified me fit to fly.

I had other ideas. I walked into the executive officer's office the day before I was scheduled to fly again for the first time since the crash and told him I wasn't going to fly any more. He seemed compassionate with me for the first ten minutes, asking me to sit down and closing the door, telling me to ignore rank and talk to him as one man to another. He didn't in reality want to discuss anything with me, he wanted to preach. He understood how I felt, that fearing that first flight again was a natural reaction and nothing to be shameful about. I told him fear and shame had nothing to do with my decision; I was not going to fly again. He ended his homily and warned me that only the Air Force could remove me from flying status. It was not my decision to make. "Yes, it is," I told him.

Our discussion ended and I was escorted down the hallway to the squadron commander's office. A captain ushered me in and then stood behind me at the rear of the room. The colonel sat behind his desk and asked me what all this business about not flying was? Didn't I know that's what we were in the business of doing? He didn't wait for a reply; he talked at me for another few minutes and concluded by asking me if I intended to fly the next day's mission. I could tell from the way he asked the question and by the captain's presence in the room, that a refusal to obey orders would have consequences. I could see how it would play out: the colonel would order me to fly the next day…I would refuse…then he would order the captain to begin court martial proceedings.

All I said was: "I haven't been feeling well, sir." The colonel slumped in his chair, opened a file and showed me a form. "The flight surgeon says there's nothing wrong with you," he said. "You're fit to fly." I looked at the form, then at the colonel and then turned to look at the captain. I repeated that I hadn't been feeling well. The colonel paused, dismissed the captain, and then told me to sit down. He rose and told me he'd be right back. On the walls hung framed photos of aircraft in flight, and on the desk sat a framed photo of the colonel's wife and children. I stood at attention when the colonel returned to the room, but he told me to sit back down. At that point he told me our discussion was off the record…it had never happened. The base legal officer had informed him that only a psychiatrist could remove me from flying status if I had been judged physically fit. He was aware of the friendship between Badger and me and noted that I was only eight months from discharge. My flight commander had told him the chances of my reenlisting were slim…I smiled at that one. It wouldn't do for any of his men to be treated by a psychiatrist, he wouldn't stand for the precedent it would set and the chain reaction he believed it would provoke. "Complete disorder," he said. "Can't have it." He said I could be reassigned to another work position within the squadron… one which would not require flying. He would do this if I granted him a concession. When he said that I swelled a bit, understanding I had gained some control of the situation. One of the instructors at Torii Station was rotating back to the states and I would replace him for the duration of my tour. That was a coup…most instructors were lifers…and I understood how far the colonel was willing to go to avoid the embarrassment of me seeking psychiatric treatment, of possibly succeeding in having my flight status revoked and others in the squadron lining up to attempt the same thing.

My schedule would be Monday through Friday, nine to five, no weekend shifts. I had to inform everyone it was a promotion, not an accommodation…I could never mention our deal outside his office. In return: no flight status, no blemishes on my record, and no trouble for him.

I accepted and for the duration of my time in the Air Force I tutored new airmen at Torii Station, coaching them through the same mistakes I had made two years before. At that moment, there was a last time, not a next time.

With Lindsay the future had been less certain. There were a few more next times and there was additional guilt and pain. Growing pains in retrospect…and I regret so much the pain I inflicted on hurt her, as well as on myself.

7

Lindsay and I were discussing the war the other night. She wondered what we had thought about from day to day when we were in Vietnam. I tried to describe the routine of going to work when I was at Kadena, of the boredom when I was at Cam Ranh. There were hundreds of days like that. Lindsay wasn't interested in actions or events, however, she wanted to know what I had thought about, and that was an epiphany for me: only the deviations from that time remain. I told her that as our time grew shorter, we thought about home…what it would be like, what it would mean to us, admitting when we were honest with one another that coming home frightened us. The uncertainty. We had to guard against thinking about home too much…it could become a dangerous pastime, could bring on depression and fear. We had seen the fear of what to do after your discharge drive more than one first-timer to reenlist. One guy I knew, married with two kids, knuckled under to pressure from the lifers and reenlisted for another four years when he was only two months from getting out. The Air Force gave him a ten thousand dollar signing bonus. It was less expensive to retain Vietnamese linguists, even at that price, than train new ones. He signed on for four more years and watched his friends fall away from him like dead leaves. That was cruel, but a fact of life. The lines were drawn and he knew what to expect. From that moment he shattered his old circle of friends, and invited lifers to occupy the new circle. I understood his anxiety, with a wife and two kids, starting over…remolding his life…scared him, but still I thought his solution was chickenshit.

All the lost memory...was there so much not worth remembering or have I blotted it out? Lindsay eventually stopped pressing me for details the other night after I asked her what she had thought from day to day when we were first married. It caught her short; I could see that in her expression. She paused at first, and then said she had thought about being in love. I laughed, which obviously displeased her. But it seemed funny to me. I recalled the deceptions as well as the joy. Making love is an intimacy, but honesty entails more...it's the pinnacle of intimacy. I have never been totally honest with Lindsay about the early years of our marriage...I don't see the point of compounding the pain I caused her at the time by rehashing it now in the name of honesty. In that same way, if I were totally honest with her about the war, how it affected me, about Badger's death...all of it unvarnished...I don't imagine she could understand. What benefit is honesty if you can't comprehend the importance of it? Maybe I'm rationalizing not confiding in her. My instinct at this point in our lives is to share everything with her. She believes she knows me so well and I'm hesitant to contradict her illusion. If I flood her with all of this, I'm not sure she'd still want me...still love me. I want to be needed and loved. Lindsay is an anchor.

That's self-defeating, though, isn't it? Lindsay is the anchor to whom I don't want to admit that I need security. I wonder if she sees that. You always condemn in others those faults you most despise in yourself. She's not a shallow woman, but I'm uncertain if I want to make the leap and open up to her. But if not to her, then whom? I divulged a lot to the VA shrink, but there was always a distance there; it's a greater gap than the one between Lindsay and me when we turn off the lights each night and lay together, snuggling, humming the same song and giggling. Having her walk out on me…there's real fear at work.

The cheating ended many years ago…Lindsay trusts me and she always loved me. That made the guilt then so acute. Betraying someone's love isn't the same as betraying their trust. As a child in Catholic school, I laughed at the notion of hell…an early non-believer. A child's logic convinced me there could not be a hell, because it seemed perfectly natural that burning couldn't last forever. I learned disrespect for authority at a young age: Catholic schools and then the Air Force, from one hierarchy to another and always the plebe. In basic training the training instructor told us the lowest scum in the world was whale shit…it settled deeper than anything else in the ocean…but if you lifted a whale turd, did we know what we'd find? "I'd find you, airman!" he'd barked. Nice folks at Lackland Air Force Base…polite, informative. My instructor was a redneck with a gold pinky ring and a pock-marked face. His hair was slicked back with Brylcreem (funny to remember that now) and he clamped his cigarette in his teeth when he smoked. He enjoyed destroying someone's self-confidence.

Badger was the first person who made me believe it was important to have a strong sense of self. I felt good about myself knowing him. I wonder if I ever felt that way before I met him or if I've felt as strong since. What I learned about myself through him helped me survive. I don't think I'm over-estimating his importance to me. Especially that night in the jungle, it's hard to imagine surviving… he kept me alive that night. When we crashed and then hung up in those trees, I concentrated on not falling to the ground. We had been warned in training not to assume how far it might be to the jungle floor. Others had misjudged and injured themselves badly, then been captured by the NVA. I didn't want to become a POW. One of the survival schools we had attended back in the states had simulated a POW camp. Barbed wire, armed guards and mock interrogations. The North Vietnamese knew what we did in our aircraft, and they wouldn't have wasted any time trying to crack us if we had been captured. It had always scared the shit out of me in the abstract, until that day when we hit the silk.

My back hurt like hell and my shoulders ached and I worried that I'd broken something. I didn't want to move but eventually catalogued my movements: from toes to feet to legs, from fingers to hands to arms. The jungle had fallen silent when we landed, and slowly the noise resumed: birds, insects, what I took for a monkey. So much chatter. At first I didn't know how close Badger was to me. When the tree tops rose up at me, I lost sight of him. The wind turned me around and I couldn't see him anymore. I couldn't see the sky through the tree canopy; I couldn't even see my entire parachute the foliage above me was so thick, but laterally there was visibility. I had no idea how far up in the trees we were hanging…it could have been ten feet or a hundred…luckily as it turned out, between two levels of forest canopy: dense green layers below and above. I listened for voices, either NVA or other crew members. When we bailed out, we scattered over several square miles of Laos. Lak Sao, near where Badger and I landed, sat right on the Ho Chi Minh trail…all this stuff I learned later during the debriefings. I made no sound…there was an excellent chance our chutes had been seen and that someone would be searching for us soon. It must have been three minutes before I heard Badger whistling. Yes, whistling. He scared the shit out of me. He was behind me so that I had to twist in my harness to see him. There he was, fifteen yards away and waving to me and smiling. What a clown, even in that bad comedy. Watching him hang there, swinging slightly, struck me as so damned funny, and so damned surreal. I think he was scared, like me; he had been in the plane as we struggled down the aisle from our compartment to the cargo ramp. By then we could feel the aircraft begin to spin counterclockwise and it struck us that if we didn't get to the ramp and bail out immediately, we'd never make it off the aircraft. His face was painted with fear as we jumped, but when I spied him in the tree, he was comical again. I started to say something but he waved me silent.

We hung there silently for an hour and a half. When I'd hear a noise below us, I'd twist myself around to look at him, but most of the time I spent facing away from him, staring off into a tunnel of limbs and leaves. When Badger whispered to me, it startled me…a human voice in that place seemed out of place. He whispered my name and I turned to look at him. He asked if I was hurt. I told him my back ached and he nodded, giving me a thumbs-up sign. I swung back to face the trees. During that hour and a half I inventoried all the gear in my harness, trying to remember where everything was. It'd been more than a year since I'd had to deal with any of it. The strobe light, the flares, the compass and knife, the radio, the beacon that automatically began signaling when my parachute opened. I had hesitated using the radio for fear of being heard from the ground. I was preoccupied with that when Badger whispered to me, and the shock of his voice confirmed where I was and how I'd gotten there. It was the longest hour and a half of my life.

I was nervous about his whispering. Although I had not heard any sounds from the jungle floor, that didn't mean there weren't NVA down there. I didn't want to take any chance that would lead to being captured. After Badger gave me the thumbs-up, we were quiet for a while. But then I heard a rustling noise, not from the ground but from

Badger's direction. I twisted around and found him eating a candy bar., and the sight of him hanging there in a parachute harness, chewing on a candy bar seemed emblematic in some sense. I had nothing to eat and would have asked him to toss me a piece, but the chances of catching it were remote, and I did not want to risk a piece of a candy bar landing at the feet of an unsuspecting NVA searcher. Badger waved at me and said I should tie off my harness above me with some of the lowering rope, so that my hands would be free and we could face one another. That seemed reasonable, so I reached behind me, to release the rope, and noticed some of my parachute lines were slack, so I cut a length of nylon from the chute and twisted myself around again, wrapped the line around the harness where the supports crossed, and tied it off securely with a square knot, and then anchored the harness to a limb beside me. That kept me from swinging away from facing Badger. The exertion brought on a new pain…in my crotch. The harness dug into my thighs, but the alternative, of lowering myself to the jungle floor, was out of the question, so I put up with the pain.

We hung silently for another hour or so waiting to hear the sound of Jolly Green engines. But we heard none. There had been time for the pilot to radio our aircraft's position before the crew bailed out and I had expected rescue teams to be near us by then. Badger reached behind into his chute pack and suddenly the crackle of a radio erupted and Badger was jerking around in his harness, trying to lower the volume. The noise sounded loud enough for everyone to hear for miles around, amplified as it was by my fear. He finally dialed down the volume, and cocked his head to listen. I leaned forward as far as I could, trying to eavesdrop…the irony of that hit for a moment. That's when I heard the noise from the ground. My first reaction was that they were footsteps on dry leaves. They sounded as though they were a good distance below us. Two hours or more hanging in a tree and the first sound I hear besides Badger is a sound I truly did not want to hear. There was no way for us to see the ground and that reassured me, since I figured no one down there could see us up here either. Badger turned off his radio and placed a finger to his lips. We both looked down and listened. I held my breath. The rustling grew fainter…it could have been an animal, but the noises of other animals around us had quieted as well. If it was an animal, it was a predator, and if it was a human predator, then Badger and I were the prey it was stalking. The feeling did not sit with me very well. After half an hour of silence, Badger turned his radio back, the volume almost inaudible. He was monitoring Guard, the distress channel, which the rescue teams would be using. After a few moments, he smiled and waved to me, circling his hand in the air like a chopper blade. Help was coming!

I wanted to shout, I was so damned relieved and happy. Then he spoke softly into the radio…contact. I couldn't believe it. The Jolly Greens were on their way. Minutes passed, and then Badger whispered something and switched off his radio. "We're hot," he whispered. But to me the words seemed to carry clearly. "What?" I asked. "The place is crawling with NVA. They want us bad."

We shut up then. Minutes passed and in my impatience, I reached for my radio and turned it on at its lowest volume, holding the tiny speaker to my ear. I overheard a Jolly Green pilot talking to another pilot, probably one of the Sandy pilots who flew rescue mission fire support. They referenced having picked up two crew members and were returning to NKP for refueling. One of the rescued men was wounded and I wondered who it was, could it be Springer? I learned later it had been the co-pilot. Springer was unharmed and was one of the first men rescued. He had come down in a clearing, but had raced to a tree line and hidden until the chopper appeared. He spent the night in a bed at the NKP infirmary while Badger and I sweated it out hanging in the jungle.

At this point we had not heard any aircraft in our area. There was more than one chopper involved in the search and rescue mission…they kept referring to themselves on the radio as Jolly Green One and Jolly Green Two. After a while I heard another referred to as Jolly Green Three. I said nothing because I was paranoid the NVA would hear us. We knew they monitored Guard, too. Jolly Green Three's signal sounded the strongest. Badger called to the pilot, giving his call sign. Communications with downed airmen had evolved into a protocol designed to protect everyone involved. Early in the war, the NVA captured downed flyers and then used their radios to lure in rescue teams, and then shot down the Jolly Greens. Airmen on combat flight status filled out a form that contained four questions; the answers, unique to each man, were used to verify identification in situations such as ours.

Badger breezed through his questions and then the pilot asked me mine.

"Where'd you go to school?"

"Memphis State."

"What's your pet's name?"

"Tony."

"What's your mother's maiden name?"

"Westley."

"Who plays shortstop for the Indians?"

"What the hell? That's not one of my questions!" I was scared to death and this guy's making jokes. He laughed and said humor sometimes made time on the ground pass a little faster. "Keep your heads down."

Badger said we were still in our harnesses, hanging in the trees and asked when we might expect extraction. The pilot told us we were probably safer where we were and warned us to limit our communications. They had a location for us, but the area was near an NVA basecamp and our pickup didn't look good for today. I looked at Badger and that's when I noticed that the light that had been penetrating the canopy above us had dimmed. It was getting darker and we both knew there would be no nighttime rescue. Jolly Green Three told us to deactivate our beacons so the NVA couldn't radio direction find us during the night. He told us to sit tight, that we'd be the first picked up in the morning, and wished us luck.

After the radio went dead, the darkness intensified and the thought of spending the night hanging there in the trees sank in, I remember wishing someone could stay on the radio and tell one-liners all night. I strained, trying to detect any sounds from below, anticipating footsteps or voices. But I was met with silence, although the sounds of the jungle filtered through to me. Badger seemed to be dozing in his tree, so I whistled softly. He raised his head and squinted at me. "What?" he called and I immediately hushed him and shook my head. We'd been in the trees for more than five hours. I was hungry, thirsty, exhausted and in pain. Remaining in the trees was the safest option. It was difficult to see Badger by then, and soon I couldn't see him at all. When I held a hand in front of my face and moved it back and forth, I couldn't see my fingers.

Total darkness…I'd never been surrounded by it before. It made me realize what a light-conscious country this is. It's damned near impossible to find anyplace here that's totally dark. Streetlights, nightlights…we're seduced by pushing back the night.

The jungle was black and the black was frightening. It wasn't merely the darkness…my sense of sight was eliminated. If there were any stars shining that night, the canopy above me shielded me from them, and it was obvious there was no moon. I saw absolutely nothing and it was an eerie fear. Each of us had flashlights in our survival packs, and strobes, but neither of us was going to risk using them and pinpoint our position to the enemy below.

Badger and I whispered sporadically that night, as an attempt to keep the fear at bay. But talking only served to remind us of how dangerous noise could be. We were both afraid. The NVA owned the night…we'd heard that time and time again. I'm sure they knew we were still in the area, even if they had not located us yet. One time we heard voices below us…talking and yelling and laughing. My linguistic skills abandoned me and all I heard were the tones of their speech. They sounded much like Badger and me and our friends sounded when cruising bars in Koza. I wondered if NVA grunts hated their own lifers. It occurred to me that only lifers should get shot down… they'd enjoy the martyrdom.

Shortly after darkness enveloped us, the anxiety began. I called quietly to Badger, mostly to reassure myself he was still there. He answered just as softly and said he was trying to get some sleep; then he giggled. He was scared and trying to cover it with humor. Something I had not anticipated was the sense of confinement the darkness could enforce. I'm claustrophobic and even in the openness of hanging in that tree, the darkness wrapped me like a quilt, as though it had substance, and I realized that if I allowed it to, the darkness would close around me tightly, constricting me. When it became too much to bear, I'd whisper to Badger and he'd respond to me calmly, almost as though he understood my need to hear his voice. He helped keep me under control, as though hearing his voice was a way of seeing him, of maintaining a safe buffer between myself and the darkness. My back ached, the insides of my thighs chafed, and I was developing a headache from eyestrain, from squinting in the darkness in an effort to see anything at all. I tried to close my eyes, but like a boy on Christmas Eve, I couldn't keep them shut. I know there was adrenalin pumping, and the fear of going to sleep and waking unprepared for an emergency also kept me awake. I was too keyed up, anxious and fearful to sleep.

The wind picked up and I began swaying in my harness like a human wind chime. I creaked and moaned on the limbs and I was certain everyone within a mile could hear me. I remembered a conversation Badger and I had had about our fathers one night in our apartment in Koza. We both felt our fathers had locked themselves into dull existences at early ages. They'd each served in World War II, and when they'd returned home had secured jobs, married, had children, bought a car and a home…from our perspective they'd done nothing more, had gone as far in life as they had chosen. But as we juxtaposed our experiences with those of our fathers, realized how they must have hungered for a life as different from the military as the two of us wanted, we thought perhaps our fathers' lives were not so empty as we supposed. Responsibilities can be limiting or liberating, we decided. My father's responsibilities liberated him and I admitted to Badger that night that I had never respected him for all he had done for his family. It had been expected of him…it was the norm… it was not extraordinary that he didn't bolt from the pack and take another path. Yet for all the conformity, it remained a choice he made, a responsibility he happily accepted. Badger and I concluded that night that nothing ever changes…each of us believes our epiphanies are original…but the cycle repeats.

I believed it could have been our fathers hanging in those trees for all the differences between us and them.

Around me there were sounds, each distinctive, but after a while they became lost in an aural hodgepodge. Tree lizards called out with a complaint like a ricocheting bullet, sounding like a firefight. When I was a child I was given a toy rifle with a sound effect built into the stock. Every time I pulled the trigger, there'd be a sound of a rifle firing and the whine of a ricochet. I loved it, thought it was unbelievably neat. But then I stopped using it in our neighborhood war games, because the sound effect meant I always missed my shot. Even as a child I understood that the object of the game of war wasn't to miss the enemy every time.

Later in the night I began to hear faint voices, not from the ground, but around me in the trees…hallucinations, I knew…but they didn't worry me. They formed speech in my imagination: I heard song lyrics and one of my old teachers lecturing about biology. They passed in and out of clarity and I wondered if I was in shock. I recalled other conversations I'd had with Badger, realizing that when he talked about what he would do when he returned to the States, he always spoke in the singular. It was always "I this" and "me that." Never "we" anything. I had asked him before if the two of us would stay in touch and he admitted he wanted a vacation from all things Air Force, from anyone and anything that would remind him of the war. Did I understand? We were great fiends but being around one another could only remind him of things he already wanted to forget.

It might be a few years before he would be ready to sit down over a beer and talk about life that had nothing to do with the war.

I had felt hurt a little, listening to him tell me that our closeness mightn't survive the war. But in the years since, I've done exactly what Badger said he would do. If he were alive today, I know we'd be in contact with one another., who knows, maybe even living in the same city. There are several of us who reconnected through email and then through Facebook. Springer and I chat online from time to time, but it's much as Badger predicted: we reminisce about the war but have no real interest in what we've done with our respective lives since.

I had difficulty judging time hanging there. I'd be certain an hour had passed, then check my watch and find no more than fifteen minutes had gone by. Late that night I tried again to sleep, but it seemed more tiring to close my eyes than it was to stay awake. I had visions of friends from high school, of guys back at Kadena, of my parents. They all talked to me in those faint voices. My father told me hanging in a tree was a stupid thing to do.

Despite the fact that it's a cliché, I will say it anyway: that night was the longest night of my life. It was endless and there seemed no way to hurry the morning. I felt mortal that night, and it shocked me. Shortly before dawn I called out to Badger several times, but he didn't answer. I imagined him asleep, passed out, the victim of a snakebite. I'm terrified of snakes and I hated the idea that one might slither down my harness straps and into my flight suit. I could not imagine trying to deal with a venomous snake on top of everything else that had happened.

I kept calling to Badger in a whisper, increasing the volume a little with each successive plea. Finally he snapped at me: "Are you trying to get us killed? Shut up!" I recognized the tone of his voice and said nothing more. I hung there in my tree like a puppet. That's what we were after all…puppets…but at that moment I truly felt the strings.

8

Several developments ushered dawn upon us: birds sang a preface, the blackness brightened to a muddy grayness, and our radios sparked to life with the voice of a forward air controller. The pain in my back and thighs persisted, joined by a headache from lack of sleep. During the night we'd heard more patrols on the ground, their frequency increasing as morning approached. I suspected our pickup would not be simple or easy. The area was still hot.

Badger waved to me when I could finally see him through the morning mist. I hoped as I looked down that ground fog lay beneath the leaves. There was a sound of rustling leaves now and then, but no voices. I was hungry and thirsty and yearned for the sound of a Jolly Green, but the FAC who spoke to us said it would be some time before we could be picked up, there was an Arc Light mission scheduled in support of our rescue some distance from our position, targeting the basecamp near Lak Sao. No aircraft could be in the area when the B-52s dropped their payloads. We'd seen Arc Light strikes from the air and I didn't much relish the idea of being on the ground in the vicinity of one. A flight of three B-52s carpet bombing an area inspires awe…if you witness it from the air and not from the ground. I asked the FAC if he had an estimate for our pick-up, but he told us to sit tight, the strike was scheduled in an hour and a half, but that he guaranteed us a hot meal later in NKP. Then he flew off to clear the area of other aircraft.

We hung there again listening to the jungle awakening. Daytime sounds differed from those at night…they seemed more muted, perhaps only because of the thinning fog around us. After half an hour

Badger asked me if I was afraid to die. His voice was barely audible, he spoke so softly. He didn't wait for a reply, he just continued, saying he hadn't ever thought he would die in this war. He said he didn't want to die and I grew scared, listening to him. My pillar was crumbling. He then said he hoped the B-52s flattened the entire area and killed every motherfucker in it. "Piss on this fucking country," he said, then unzipped his flight suit, gripped his dick and peed on the leaves below us. It sounded like rain. Then the FAC called on the radio to tell us the B-52s were on line with the target area, half an hour out, and wished us good luck. It was a nice gesture but provided little reassurance. Sooner than we expected, we heard and felt the explosions. The noise, like giants drumming on our skulls, surrounded us. The trees shook, shedding leaves, and the ground quaked. The thunder started some distance from us, but then started to approach our location, and my fear escalated nearly to panic. It was like sobering up before a bar fight begins. I looked at Badger and saw he was screaming, but I couldn't hear the sound of his voice over the bomb detonations. As suddenly as the strike and its fury had begun, it ended, leaving echoes in its absence. Badger stopped screaming and just stared at me with eyes so empty I couldn't tell if he even recognized me.

We hung there in the aftermath, gently swinging in our harnesses and a feeling of total control infused me. That should have been Badger's role…he was always the voice of reason…but he appeared lost, as though he had either slipped away or back into himself. He looked meek. I was the one in control now, I realized. I indicated for him to remain quiet, and he nodded. I knew the chopper would come in to get us soon; they'd want to move in as quickly after the raid as possible, while the NVA were busy recovering from the strike. Badger gripped the straps of his harness, his mouth set tightly. It started to rain, pelting the canopy above us with a sound like bacon sizzling. I tilted my head back and allowed rainwater to fill my mouth, but Badger hung his head forward and let the water wash over the back of his head. I wanted to reach across the divide and slap his face.

The FAC radioed that the Jolly Greens were en route with an ETA of twenty minutes. Air support was accompanying the choppers and he figured we'd be out and back on friendly ground in about an hour. He asked our situation and I replied that we were hungry, but otherwise fine. He said the area was still considered hot, the pickup might be hairy, but the air support was going to make it tough on the NVA. Badger said nothing and that made me angrier than before. We were an hour from safety and he was moping like a child. I contemplated yelling something at him when I heard the voices. They were Vietnamese and they were close. The rain made hearing anything specific difficult, but there was definitely a patrol in the area, not far from us. I raised a finger to my lips as I looked at Badger, and he nodded, with his arms slack at his sides. The voices, several of them now, sounded farther away than when I had first heard them, and fearing they might hear my radio, I lowered the volume as much as I dared. There were men, quite a few of them, walking below us, hurriedly talking to each other. Then there was a gunshot, a rifle fired up into the branches, and I heard it strike a limb twenty yards away. Badger laughed quietly and I hissed at him to shut up. There was silence below us and then more rifle shots fired into the trees, but still some distance from us. The fog had slowly been thinning and as I looked down I noticed gaps in the canopy below us…leaves on the lower limbs had fallen during the Arc Light mission, and patches of the jungle floor were visible.

Badger chuckled again, quietly, but it frightened and angered me. I heard a shout from the ground and then more rifle shots, getting nearer, the bullets spitting through the trees like angry hornets buzzing toward the sky. I panicked and twisted in my harness as I surveyed the canopy directly below me. My cover seemed undisturbed and sufficient to shield me from eyes on the ground. I heard voices again, right below us, the clicking of rifle bolts, magazines slapped into the weapons, and then bullets seemed to be swarming all around us. I swung in my harness and grabbed for a tree limb, clutching it and trying to maneuver it between me and the ground. But I couldn't keep a grip. I swung back again, unsuccessfully. All I could do was hang there and hope to God I wasn't hit. Badger continued his low chuckle and the voices drifted closer to a spot below him. I wanted to yell for him to shut up, but I knew if I did we'd both be killed. In that instant it occurred to me that Badger was going to be shot. I saw chunks of bark flying off the tree limbs around him, but he continued to laugh softly. The entire scene was farcical but there was no way I could laugh…I could barely breathe, watching him hang there with bullets rifling past him. Then the first bullet hit him. In his right leg. It ripped a swatch from his flight suit and blood stained the material around the wound. He never stopped his faint laughter. An automatic weapon stitched a pattern in a tree trunk behind him. More bullets plowed through the limbs; the second and third bullets hit him… in the hand and the side, jerking him in his harness. Another struck him in his chest, creating a wound the size of a coffee cup. He wasn't laughing any more. The shooting continued for a minute or two more, then stopped. No more laughing, no more killing. Badger hung there dead, frothy blood dripping from his mouth. I felt wetness on my chin and was afraid I'd been wounded as well, but when I put my hand to my face I felt only tears. The NVA still moved below but hadn't fired any more shots. I was terrified they would climb the tree to retrieve Badger's body, but they didn't. They wandered around for a time and then moved off.

When the FAC called to say the Jolly Greens were two minutes out, I answered with my callsign and told him there'd been ground fire from a patrol. He asked the patrol's location and I told him they had moved to the southwest. He would mark the approximate area with smoke and let the Sandys have a run at them. Then I told him that Badger was dead, using his callsign. The radio was silent for a moment and the FAC said he could see the Jolly Greens and the Sandys. He radioed one of the chopper pilots, alerting him to the fact that there was one pickup and one KIA. As the chopper pilot called me, I reached down to a pocket in my pants leg and grabbed my knife. I cut the cord I had tied around my harness to keep me facing Badger as I talked with the chopper pilot. The sound of the engines grew closer and I heard the FAC give the Sandy pilots some coordinates and tell them to lay down some gravel. I had no idea what he was talking about, but they told me later they were mining the area west of me to keep the NVA from doubling back while the chopper picked me up. The chopper pilot asked my situation and I told him how I was hanging in tree limbs. They'd lower a penetrator, he said, the sound of the chopper close enough now to make hearing the radio difficult. Moments later he told me to pop smoke, so I dug out a smoke canister from my harness, tugged at the ring and held it away from my body as red smoke rose through the limbs. The pilot said "Roger. We've marked your smoke, what color is it?" "Red," I replied. The Jolly Green edged closer and the leaves and limbs around me swirled as the wash of the blades whipped everything around me. As limbs bent in the wind, I could see the chopper above me; in the doorway a man gripped a machine gun and another guy guided the jungle penetrator down toward me. It fell lower and lower and dangled only a few feet out of my reach. He maneuvered it closer to me while the pilot kept the chopper hovering in place. Finally I reached out and grabbed it. I folded down the leg supports, straddled it, and then unsnapped myself from my parachute harness. I signaled them to hoist me up. Limbs scraped at my face as they raised me, and suddenly small arms fire erupted from below and to the west. I heard gunfire and explosions and the screams of the Sandy's engines as they raced by at low altitude. I nuzzled my face in the crook of my elbow, letting the branches slide over my back, and as I twirled on the penetrator cable, I saw Badger's tree. He hung there like a goddamned puppet, dangling in his harness, swaying in the chopper wash, as gunfire came closer, bullets slashing through the trees, and then I was out of the canopy, in the air. It was overcast and the chopper seemed like a giant. The gunner was firing down into the jungle as a crewmember pulled me into the chopper, then leaned over and asked me about the other guy. I said he was dead. He radioed the pilot that there was KIA down there, listened and shook his head, then leaned down to me and said the area was too hot. They were pulling out. The gunner continued to fire as a medic strapped me down onto a stretcher. The chopper rose, banking to the south, picking up altitude. The gunner ceased firing and the only noise I heard after that was the engine and the rotors.

After ten minutes the copilot came back and asked how things were. The crewmembers gave him a thumbs-up. He asked if I was in much pain; I shrugged and said my back hurt. The medic gave me an injection and we flew back to NKP.

In three days I returned to Kadena, where I lay in a hospital bed for some time. I'd seen Springer at the NKP infirmary; he said nothing when he heard about Badger.

They never retrieved Badger's body. I signed an affidavit in NKP testifying I had seen him die so he wouldn't be listed as an MIA. Bureaucratically, I killed Badger.

I felt rotten when I returned to Kadena. I lay in bed, in traction, while a parade of friends and lifers marched past, muttering empty lines of grief and concern. They fawned over me and tried to be considerate of my feelings, but I retreated into myself. Only Springer seemed to empathize, but even when he and I sat together, we were mostly silent. How could I explain to him that Badger killed himself? Or that I was not responsible? I'm not to blame…no one is guilty…everyone is guilty. All those times Badger and I spoke of returning home, of getting back to the world. I remember stories of veterans who never adjusted…home revealed itself as a place more fucked up for them than the war. Nothing makes sense here and nothing made sense over there. I clung for so long to feeling that way. I wonder if Badger feared coming home, as though he sensed that looking for a solid foundation for life after the war would only lead to the disappointment of standing on wet sand.

Last week a guy at the bar pulled a knife. Mary, an old regular, was seated at the bar with her afternoon Scotch when this guy walked in and ordered a pitcher of beer and two glasses. I figured someone was meeting him, got his beer, and when I tried to return his change, he told me to keep it. Thank you and a nod. Mary had turned to look at the guy, then turned back to me and snorted. She ordered another Scotch and began again to tell me about her son, a familiar and favorite topic of hers. The guy from the bar walked to jukebox, fed it some bills and selected some songs. He asked me if I could turn up the volume, and I did. Mary started talking louder over the music and then this guy, who obviously didn't want to listen to Mary, asked me to turn the music up even louder. I did, but Mary's voice got even louder and it sparked an escalating argument. I told him I couldn't turn the music up any louder and that upset him. Mary laughed at him…he demanded to know what she was laughing at…called her a bitch…she called him a bastard. Suddenly he was behind her, screaming; she ignored him and then he whipped out a knife, saying he was going to cut her. Mary froze but I swung the bottle of Scotch directly into this guy's face. It shattered, he dropped the knife, and fell to the floor, covering his face with his hands. I rounded the bar with the bottle neck in my hand, dialing 911 on my cell phone with the other.

The cops arrived before the ambulance, handcuffed the guy and took my statement. Mary enjoyed one more Scotch on the house and then went home. I cleaned up the mess…there was blood, Scotch and glass all over the floor. I remembered the guy had asked for two glasses, but no one else ever showed up looking for him. That's when I decided to stop bartending. I don't need the aggravation…something my father used to say whenever we kids screwed up. "I don't need this aggravation!" He was paranoid we'd give him an ulcer, so he overcompensated and stopped worrying, especially about the things he should have.

I'm like him I suppose. I've overcompensated to the point of not caring about the things I should have tended to. The VA shrink said I'd made great progress by the time I stopped seeing her. When we first began our sessions, I avoided the truth at times and lied at others. She compared my deceit to a story about a man who digs a hole and then refills it with dirt. The mound of dirt is higher than the ground around it. He asks another man what he should do about it. "It's obvious," he says. "Dig a deeper hole."

Yesterday afternoon, when I got home from the bar, I walked into the house, hung my coat up in the closet, as I've done for years, went into the kitchen, snooping in the refrigerator for some food, and decided to change clothes. At the bottom of the stairs, I gripped the handrail and slowly took each step, contouring the palm of my hand to the shape of the banister. All the way upstairs I skimmed dust from the sides of the handrail, and when I reached the second-floor landing I looked at my hand…it was sooty from all the dust. I got a dust rag and a can of spray wax and I shined every crevice in that banister. I stood at the top of the stairs and gazed down at the length of gleaming wood and felt proud of what I'd accomplished. Working at the bar doesn't bring that sense of pride. It was the first time in so long that I'd felt that sense of gratification…not since college. Epiphanies don't fire warning shots. I sensed a changing attitude, a shift in purpose.

When Lindsay came home from work last night, she found me seated on the floor of the living room playing old records…vinyl, not CDs…my "war music," songs we had played during that time, weeping. She was so loving. She held me and told me all would be right with such conviction. I had to explain that I was crying joyful tears, and I laid out my plan, as fantastic as it sounded for a man in his sixties, to return to school, in Far Eastern studies. Perhaps as a form of atonement?

Just as my relationship with Lindsay changed so many years ago, I sense it is going to change again. More passion, more attention to her needs, less dwelling on my own problems.

I joined the Air Force when I was nineteen years old. I had no idea what I was doing, but I knew I wanted to get away from home. Until the day we were shot down, I'd never seen the war. I wasn't a grunt. I lived in what grunts would have called a country club: hot food, air-conditioned barracks in the tropical heat. I drew combat pay and threw it at booze and hookers in Okinawa. What I was doing never bothered me so much that I considered standing on my principles and refusing to do it. I played a part, a small part I rationalized, but enough of one to earn membership in an exclusive club to which I both wanted and hated being a member. I've met other vets, grunts, who watched their friends die, have taken the measure of their suffering, and felt guilty in comparison, apart from them in some desperate sense.

Last night I also showed Lindsay a black and white photograph of Badger and me taken on the beach at Cam Ranh Bay. The sun was in our eyes and we squinted above our smiles with our arms draped on each other's shoulders; the bay stretched away behind us. She asked if I still missed him, and I nodded. Then I turned to her, took her face in my hands and said: "I used to envy him."

Selected Short Stories

Grayson's Dreams

Along the length of the tree-lined street, the tiny front lawns trimmed at the sidewalks, the grass as green as still swamp water, the women stood at their doorways, some in housecoats, others in skirts and blouses or baggy slacks, shaking their heads, indicating the man had not hidden in their homes. Staring from woman to woman, Grayson sensed his hope sinking and his anger swelling; he turned, his fists clenched so tightly his knuckles whitened, and confronted his own house, with the corner porch screened against the summer insects, the wood trim around the windows flaking white paint chips to the driveway, the brick walls rough and fading from the red hue of years before to a dull brown. He advanced up the steps, across the porch and vestibule to the living room, across the carpet and around the settee to the stairs, bounding two steps at a stride, pausing at the landing to listen, and hearing no sound whatsoever, walking deliberately down the corridor to the bedroom where his wife lay sleeping upon the mattress. Grayson chose not to wake her. He pivoted from the room and retraced his steps down the corridor to the bathroom, where a foreboding chill beckoned to him from the shower stall. His steps across the narrow room seemed sluggish as he grasped the shower curtain and yanked it back; the man leaped from his crouch, his arms flailing at Grayson, the curtain tangled between the two men. The rod tore from its foundation in the walls. They wrestled, the curtain wrapping itself around them both like a blanket. Every rapist deserves to die, Grayson told himself, driving on towards the man's eyes with the fingers of one hand, the other tightening around the man's throat.

Grayson hunched his back as the man railed desperate blows on Grayson's back and shoulders.

Another dream, a bout of sweating anger, waking with the bed sheet knotted between his legs, and his wife, Kate, shying to the far side of the bed, avoiding the arms flung at his imaginary foe.

Awareness, like syrup, oozed over Grayson's consciousness as he ceased his struggling, bent his legs and pulled them to his chest, circling them with his arms; he tilted forward and rested his forehead, slick and greasy, on his knees. Breathing deeply he turned his head toward Kate. His wife crouched at the mattress edge, an expression of weary understanding visible in her eyes, and Grayson wondered at the depth of her patience. For the past week the same or similar dreams had plagued his nights, rapists and revenge, until the prospect of sleep conveyed a fear, not of the dream itself, but of its inconclusiveness, of the frustration Grayson experienced from what he regarded as premature awakening. Always in a sweat, always moments before he killed the man.

Gray light shone outside the bedroom windows and the digital clock on the oak table which Kate had refinished the previous summer read six-ten. Grayson managed a slight smile for his wife, then rolled his eyeballs upward in their sockets, as though to express again his apology for the disruption of her sleep. The unpredictable accepted as routine was what he realized he had come to expect of her, and again Grayson wondered at the depth of her patience

"Same dream? Kate asked.

Grayson stretched out his legs and laid his head back on the foam rubber pillow, staring at the ceiling, noting a cobweb threading along the crown molding.

"Just about,'" he answered his wife.

"Think you can get back to sleep?"

"I'll give it a try," Grayson said as he untangled the bed sheet and spread it across both he and Kate as she lay down beside him and caressed his chest with her hand.

"I love you," she whispered.

"I know you do, Kate. I know you do," Grayson whispered in return, the genuineness of the emotion triggering a sudden inhalation.

He lay on his back, the royal sleeping position he recalled from some distant memory, particulars of the dream nagging his consciousness, staving off sleep as the gray light beyond the curtained windows brightened with dawn. Beside him Kate's breathing steadied into the rhythm so familiar it had become a soothing lullaby for him. But its calming effects failed as his eyes refused to remain shut, the lids fluttering open, keeping pace with his concerns. Faint rumblings of early morning traffic from the interstate wafted on a breeze which ballooned the curtains inward from the windows. Birds chattered in the trees and shrubs and Grayson heard the shower running in his next-door neighbor's bathroom. He had always believed the houses in this old neighborhood had been placed too close to one another. Every month when he wrote out the check for the mortgage payment, he reasoned for such a sum, no man should be subjected to a view of his neighbors. How much must he pay for insulation? Insulation from the press of others' problems. Insulation from the plague of this dream.

Grayson rolled to his side, a sleeping position for which he could recall no name, if even one existed, and eyed a crack in the wall plaster, tiny and irregular, tracing its fractured path to the windowsill. Another cobweb. Restlessness, whether induced by the dream or Grayson's habitual dissatisfaction with the house, animated his limbs as though some unseen puppeteer had yanked crucial strings. He swung his legs off the bed, rose to a sitting position and turned to view his wife. Kate slept undisturbed as Grayson rose and tiptoed from the room. He strode down the corridor to the spare bedroom at the rear of the house, where he sat on a walnut chair before a desk, another piece Kate had stripped and refinished that summer. He held in his hands the contracts which had been delivered by special messenger the week before. Kate had not yet signed them.

A San Francisco firm, financed with Japanese capital, sought to franchise Kate's shop. A generous cash settlement for the rights to the shop name and concept, in addition to Kate's appointment as a vice-president, would erase Grayson's money worries for the rest of their lives.

Yet Kate permitted the contracts to age on the desk, Grayson's and her secure future lacking merely her signature upon the copies. Just a slight scratch of the pen, Grayson thought, and every headache associated with the shop and its operation vanishes...someone in San Francisco earns the ulcers.

At the end of the block a garbage truck turned into the alley behind the row of houses, its diesel engine complaining with a rumble as it wheezed to a halt and discharged its driver. Grayson gazed out the window with a vacant stare, his mind visualizing the pleasant, neighborless view from their new home, a vista of towering evergreens and lush meadows sloping toward the sea, or perhaps a mountain lake as clear and brilliantly blue as a cornflower. His dream world in which he might be free of dreams. The placidity of Grayson's fantasy shattered beneath the sudden awareness that he had not put out by the garbage cans the box of rags and empty paint cans the night before. The truck ground its way down the alley toward the house, and Grayson raced to the bedroom, where he speedily donned a pair of jeans, slipped his feet into thonged sandals and sped down two flights of stairs to the basement.

The box was cumbersome because of its bulk and not from any great weight, a carton in which books had been shipped to the shop, now piled high with empty paint cans and rags starched with dried paint. Grayson's nostrils prickled at the smell of the kitchen, the unmarred walls a pale green, the odor of paint not as heady as last night, but still forceful. He balanced the box on his hip and swung open the back door, unlocked the screened door, then angled through the doorway, pushing against the screen with a corner of the box. The door ripped with a sound like an old man clearing his throat, and the frame closed against Grayson, a section of the screen folded around the box like wrapping paper. Grayson cursed under his breath and pushed against the doorframe, sidling outside with the box edge cutting into his thigh. If it's not one thing with this house, it's another, he thought. Scuffing through the dewy grass, he carried the carton across the yard to the gate in the rear fence. The garbage truck, its exhaust charcoal against the silver sky, idled three houses down the alley. A man in grimy denim overalls and a ruffled shirt with the sleeves cut off, disappeared behind the truck, carrying a large, gray plastic tub, bulging with Grayson's neighbors' refuse. Leaning over the waist-high plank fence, Grayson lowered the box to the patch of gravel beside his trash cans. He stared at the paint cans and stiffened rags, recalling the argument with Kate over the wisdom of painting the kitchen. Her stubbornness in the matter still rankled him, and when at last fatigue dictated his surrender to her insistence, a new conflict arose with Kate's selection of colors. Grayson could not in all his memories remember a pale green kitchen; yellow, pink, or white, these were the colors of kitchens. Once, in a cousin's home in New Hampshire, he had entered a two-tone blue kitchen, robin's egg on the walls with navy trim on the cabinets and woodwork. And all her dishes, Pfaltzgraff Yorktowne stoneware...blue and white everywhere. But never green. Pale green. Paler than the newest spring leaf; paler than any St. Patrick's Day affectation he could recall. With each brush stroke Grayson had balked, wondering why Kate's fix-it-up fever burned so intensely, when her signature on the contracts resting on the desk upstairs could hire as many professional painters as she could possibly want, each and every one of them matching colors and hues to swatches of material from the new furniture, new walls in their new home.

The diesel engine coughed and Grayson looked up to see the man halt the garbage truck by the edge of Grayson's property. He climbed down from the high cab and stared at Grayson, then hefted his tub on his shoulder and walked toward a row of trash cans. Witnessing the man at so close a distance triggered within Grayson's memory a withered notion, that insight could be gleaned from conversation with a working class man. Somehow, the adage promised, people who labored with their hands divined answers to profound questions of purpose: Why love? Why live? Simple solutions evolved from a simple existence. Grayson recognized the fallacy of such an idealistic supposition, admitting his life at present seemed complex simply because his own aspirations remained outside his grasp; in all honesty, Grayson had relinquished determination of the future to Kate...and the franchise contracts.

"You got something you wanna say to me, mister?"

The words shocked Grayson out of his thoughts, and he raised his head to confront the man. What Grayson had assumed was the man's hair now revealed itself as a black kerchief bound around his head and knotted at the back of the man's neck. Pocketing his hands and stepping back from the fence, Grayson shook his head.

"No, No. Just getting some air, that's all."

The man eyed Grayson, then lifted the box of paint cans and rags and tossed it into his plastic tub.

"Lots better air somewhere else than garbage cans."

Grayson nodded and turned back toward the house, the sun tinting the eastern sky with an orange haze. Scarcely nine hours earlier, Grayson had been at the driving range, caged behind the wheel of an aging Ford tractor, dragging a contraption like an old rotary mower in ever-tightening circles, the blades slapping the yellow golf balls into twin bins. Duffers under the lights on the Astroturf tees cheered whenever a drive rattled Grayson's wire cage.

In the bedroom Grayson stripped off his jeans and slipped off his sandals, his feet wet from the dew. Kate slept on her side, one arm crooked as a pillow beneath her head, her hair fallen over half her face. Grayson gripped her shoulder and shook her. Kate muttered and twisted away to evade his grasp, but Grayson shook her more firmly.

"What is it?" Kate whined as she rolled and propped herself on her elbows, squinting at Grayson seated beside her on the mattress.

"Are you awake enough to understand me, Kate?" Grayson said. "It's important that you understand what I have to say to you."

Kate nodded her head.

"No, you have to answer me. I want to know that you'll remember what I'm going to say."

"I'm awake," Kate bristled, and sharply sat up.

"All right, now listen to me," Grayson inhaled deeply. "Those contracts have been sitting on that desk for over a week now. I think that's long enough. You make a decision today. You sign them this morning, or you send them back, okay?"

Kate said nothing, merely tilted back her head until it softly thumped against the headboard.

"I'm serious, Kate. You sign them today or you send them back.

Fingering the hem of her nightgown, Kate turned to her husband. "If that's what you want, Grayson."

"You know what I want."

"All right."

Grayson leaned over and kissed his wife, then laid down beside her and covered himself with the bed sheet. As the garbage truck in the alley droned in compression of its cargo, Grayson pressed his eyes shut and waited to fall asleep, tension in the form of a tightening of the muscles at the back of his neck reminding him of the frustration of his incomplete dream. Perhaps this one time, he thought, just this one time, I'll kill him.

Koi Pond

I draped my suit coat on a fence post and retrieved a short-handled fish net and a five-gallon plastic bucket from the garage. Sitting on the capstones of the pond wall, I stared at the four koi languidly swimming. The fountain bubbled in the center of the pond, the water splashing back down like frenzied percussion.

Our house sets across a tree-lined street from a public park dominated by a shaded lagoon, which freezes in winter, hosting hockey games and neighborhood skating; during the summer children and adults fish for bass and catfish beneath its gentle willows. When we bought our two-story Victorian, we installed a modest pond in the tiny backyard and stocked it with three-inch-long butterfly koi. They are beautiful, graceful fish, their silky scales patterned in splotches of glittering orange, luminous ebony and creamy white, their fanlike tails swiftly propelling them with an elegance attainable only in water. Having grown plump on twice-daily feedings, they now measure nearly eighteen inches in length. My wife read that their life expectancies could exceed fifty, even seventy years.

On the patio beside the pond, dark emerald moss thrived between the slabs of New York bluestone. Several times over the years, when I wearied of the persistent maintenance and care of the pond and the measures I undertook to protect the fish from marauding raccoons, I threatened to dump the koi into the lagoon in the park across the street, but my wife consistently forbade it. She named each of the fish, assuming I could never countenance watching a named fish hooked and snatched from the lagoon by some eager angler.

I dipped the bucket into the pond, filling it with murky water. The smell was pungent and primal, evidence that I've been neglecting the pond. Many of the water hyacinths and lilies have browned and need pruning. Tracking Smudge, the fish with the brilliant orange blemish behind its head, I whisked it with a swooshing motion from the pond and released its squirming form into the bucket. My body leaned from the weight as I lurched down the driveway, straining to keep the water from sloshing over the edge of the bucket. The oak beside the house had shed its leaves and last night's rain plastered them to the concrete like an autumnal quilt.

At the lagoon's edge I lowered the bucket into the shallow water, tipping it until Smudge slithered away in a flash of iridescence and disappeared into the deeper water. Three times I repeated this trip, turned off the fountain, and then returned the bucket and the net to the garage, pausing before closing the door to dry my hands on a golf towel.

Back in the house, I removed my shoes and slumped onto one of the two matching leather armchairs in the living room and listened to the imperfect silence of an empty house.

My Dear Paul,

March 8th

My Dear Paul,

The crate arrived yesterday, battered, yet intact. None of the pieces was broken, for which I am greatly relieved.

The snows are melting, gorging the gutters with rivers of slushy mud...I love it! Richie, the neighborhood's most accomplished eight-year-old engineer, replicated Hoover Dam beside the driveway entrance Monday with Charlie Cottle from across the street. Their lake extended along the curb from our house down to the corner. Nearly every child on the block floated a boat on the surface, fashioned from scraps of wood and the Styrofoam cushioning from your last package. It reminded me of the Spanish Armada, all those children skipping along the shore, prodding their stick boats and chunks of jaggedly hacked foam.

Richie misses you, more noticeably when a shipment arrives than any other time; he asks how you are while I sit and read your letters, and pesters me so incessantly about you, that after I've shooed him out of the room, I have to begin with the first line and reread all the pages. The boy keeps asking when his Uncle Paul is going to visit again. He still talks excitedly of your stay last summer. You're a folk hero to the boy, and the pedestal he's put you on grows more precipitous every day. I'm worried, it towers so high that the only way to come down may be to fall.

Of course, his father still regards you as a fool, but I've spoken with Tom numerous times, and he's agreed to temper his remarks about you around Richie. The other night, though, as the two of us lay in bed reading, Tom rolled on his side and asked me what my crazy brother was trying to prove. I had to smile, Paul, because I suppose that's the way Tom looks at it: as though you're trying to prove something. The whole family believes you always had something to prove, as though your only motivation in life is a need to show what you're capable of, no matter what the cost. Nothing lends more credence to their arguments than that crazy car stunt of yours when we were kids. When I told Richie that his uncle, when he was eight years old, had once driven Grampa's car by wiring stilts to his feet to reach the pedals, and sitting on three telephone books till he could barely see through the steering wheel at what lay ahead of him on the streets, Tom cursed, sure that Richie would try to duplicate the event, smashing the Chevy against the maple in the front yard in the process. Richie, awed by the tale, quite perceptibly guessed his Grampa's reaction to the incident, whereupon Tom assured him the same would be in store for Richie if he tried something as stupid as that. Richie smiled, causing Tom a bit of palpitation, I'm sure.

While Tom may feel that living in northern Manitoba is foolhardy, he hungrily anticipates your packages as much as Richie and I do. Even during the most sluggish periods at the gallery, your pieces seem to sell, and Tom knows it. He simply isn't quite sure why you, even though he has learned to deal with what he calls the "artistic temperament," feel it necessary to seclude yourself among the bison and the caribou. He regards you as a bit of a prima donna, and feels you could easily work in Chicago, New York or San Francisco like the rest of your "Brethren." His word not mine. But he doesn't begrudge you his commissions, and bristles whenever I remind him of that.

You didn't mention Beth in your letter, any reason? Is she well? Is she there? Is she alive? I'm not trying to pry, at least not too overtly, but Paul, your scoreboard at romance is not impressive, and from what you wrote of Beth, I thought perhaps you'd found someone who could tolerate you long enough to fall in love with you. If you've botched it, then why not take a break, just brood in your cabin for a while. Winnipeg isn't a shopping mart for women; you can't expect to snag a new partner every time you traipse down there on a binge, then drag her back to a three-room cabin, monopolizing her every day until she's so fed up that she's willing to walk out of the woods on her own. Hell, I'm being sisterly again, elder-sisterly. You know your own mind better than I, I'm simply trying to demonstrate that I care, that's all.

Okay, time to wind up...

***don't forget Richie's birthday is the 12th of next month, he'd die if you didn't at least send a card.

***Tom will transfer the funds from the sale of the latest pieces to your bank, even though he'll probably grumble a bit as he does.

***and there's a standing invitation for you to emerge like one of your darling grizzlies, from your lair, to come and visit us whenever you want.

We all send our love, Paul, take care of yourself.

Susan

April 20th

My Dear Paul,

You're amazing! Richie loved the caribou, and even Tom admitted it was your best piece yet. I am continually amazed at how you can fashion such intricate detail. Richie sped out to show it all to his friends, especially Charlie Cottle; I don't think the two of them have been getting along very well since Charlie discovered girls. Richie's still a bit young for that sort of thing, thank God!

Janet sounds pleasant, but she also sounds amazingly similar to Beth, and before her, Linda...why don't you simplify things for both of us, and merely give them one name, say...Jayne, then number them sequentially: Jayne 1, Jayne 2, Jayne 3. I hear prospectors used to do that with their mules. It seems appropriate to you, too.

Tom says he realizes you don't need more money, but he feels what he's been charging for your pieces is insufficient, so he raised the prices a bit -- even an artist must keep pace with inflation, Paul.

And Tom says he will not lower the prices, he says you're becoming more well known all the time, and if the prices don't keep pace with your fame, no one will buy any of your work anymore. It's a paradox, he says: no one will judge you famous unless your work is high-priced. You'll have to learn to live with it, Tom says, and he suggests you use the extra money to construct a wing on your cabin, or install rudimentary plumbing. He had several other facetious suggestions, but I don't think I'll burden you with my husband's tiring sense of humor.

Well, since you raised the subject in your letter, I'll address it, but only briefly, because I don't want to belabor an issue which may lead to a schism between us. If you sincerely want someone else besides Tom to handle your work, that's a decision for you to make...but to expect me to recommend someone to you is asking too much. I mean, Paul, the gallery does put the food on my table and the clothes on my back, and if Tom ever got wind of what you wanted me to do, he'd toss me out on my ear. I think it's unfair of you to maneuver me this way. Tom has done quite nicely by you, yes, but he has also kept you in the position to maintain your hermitage with relative ease. I don't mean to appear selfish, but I think you owe it to Tom to discuss this with him, not simply parlay about it behind his back, and especially not, my God, with me.

Make your own decision.

I've got to go now, a lot to do today, including writing the folks and letting them know you haven't become some grizzly's dessert yet. Your insistence on not writing them is juvenile, do you realize that? Forget that, I don't want to resurrect any old ghosts.

Plan on visiting us this summer, won't you? You know we all want to see you, and all of us love you.

Susan

May 12th

My Dear Paul,

Of course, yes! We'll clean the house, leave the lawn untended so you'll feel more at home, and possibly even launder the sheets you slept between last year!

Richie is ecstatic! It's difficult to force him to speak of anything but your visit. The child is a born braggart, and now the entire neighborhood knows that his uncle, the famous sculptor, will be visiting after school's out. I'm afraid his sense of time still revolves around summer vacation.

Tom says the recently arrived pieces are selling well, and he instituted another price increase, slighter than the last, but he wanted me to let you know. The funds will be transferred as usual.

Mom called the other night and when I told her you would be here in June, she said perhaps she and Dad would fly out for a weekend. I said she should wait until I had a chance to speak with you, I don't want any damned feuding going on while you're here. It's trying enough to be the sole member of the family you still deign to speak with, without having something I do alienate you from me. But I do believe five years is a long enough time for them to ascertain the sincerity of your intent, and that seeing them again would not kill you. Mind you, I'm not saying they'll be here, that decision is yours...I put Mom on hold, and that's where she'll stay until you get here. Then you can determine if you want to see them. They're growing older, Paul, and they love you, regardless of what you may think. All they want to do is see you! I don't think they're asking terribly much. That's my opinion, I'm sure you have yours.

Tom has arranged the travel plans for you, with a flight out of Winnipeg on the 5th. I've enclosed the tickets both to and from; maybe you can have Jayne number whatever drive you down, or even come with you, you know she's welcome, whatever her name may be by next month.

Anyway, I'm off to help Tom at the gallery this afternoon. enjoy getting out of the house.

We all love you, take care of yourself and see you soon.

Susan

August 7th

Paul:

I'm still so embarrassed, it's difficult...let's simply say there have been many more enjoyable and effortless tasks for me in this life than writing to you again. Within me writhes a jumble of feelings, a tangle of conflicting emotions, and part of me screams that you never be forgiven for what you did. But another part demands that I accept my share of the guilt, I should not discard you as the rest of the family has done. By all rights, I should have foreseen the complications your visit would pose, and I accept my complicity, however tacit, in what happened.

I can accept the sudden shift from the gallery to Carello's. Emil's shop is larger, more prestigious, and of course, it is in New York. But honestly, Paul, you could have prepared Tom for the news a little more carefully. You may find him unamiable, you may not disguise your antagonism for him very deeply, but Paul, he worked diligently for you, and in many ways, without Tom you wouldn't have risen a bit of interest in your work from Emil. I know it's not the wisest thing to do, mixing business with family, but I think you owed Tom more than a cursory remark at dinner that you were abandoning his gallery. It was cold, it was cruel, and he has every right to remain furious with you...which he is.

As for Mom and Dad, I telephoned after you left and explained as best I could...but I don't think they bought my story. Mom heard you when you shouted across the room to me, she knew you didn't want to speak with them, and they only called to say hello. It hurt them very much.

Did you know that Dad has been ill? Or would that bit of news have altered your decision?

This an old and ancient argument, Paul, and I won't presume to belabor it with you anymore; you do as you please, send your work to Emil in New York, shun the rest of the family as though they were diseased, dismiss Tom with an aside as though he means nothing to your success...you do as you damned well please.

But...there's always a but, isn't there little brother? But...my son. That boy worshipped the ground you walked on, he idolized you! And you absolutely crushed him. I only hope he recovers from the entire incident, he's been in a funk since you left, and nothing Tom or I can do has been able to lift him out of it. What could you have been thinking? Have you been apart from civilized people so long that your brains have eroded? Are there no children in Manitoba? This is not Winnipeg, Paul, where you can recover from your binges in some cheap hotel room, with your latest Jayne beside you in the morning to shock you into sobriety.

Richie begged me to promise that you would sleep in his bed while you stayed with us. Does that impress you at all? He prayed to be able to boast to his friends that his uncle had slept in his bed while he visited. Tom retrieved the boy's sleeping bag from that attic so that Richie would be able to "camp out" on the floor beside you. He's only nine years old! He's terribly impressionable! And he loved you like a father...do you know that Tom always envied the relationship you enjoyed with Richie? Maybe some good has come of that night, now Tom can assume that position with Richie, that position which was yours.

Only I fear Richie will never again open himself to that sort of relationship, not even with his father...because you hurt him so keenly.

Tom fired Julie from the gallery, perhaps out of vindictiveness, although he says she was incompetent...perhaps I'm making excuses and rationalizing her dismissal, but Tom and I agreed it would not be healthy for Richie to encounter the woman every time he came to the gallery. So she went.

What you did was horrible, inexcusable and detrimental to a degree we can't yet fully measure. And I should have seen it developing. But even so, if there is any lingering effect on Richie, Paul, I'll write you off like the rest of them have.

What could you have been thinking, if you were thinking at all? To take that woman into Richie's room! I hope she was good, Paul, she had better have been the best you ever had. How could you speak to him as you did? I'm growing irrational again, Paul, as I do nearly every time I think about that night. To laugh at the boy and speak to him as you did. Why didn't you simply cut out his heart? It would have been just as painless.

Oh, Paul! I suppose what irritates me the most is the culpability I feel for not having anticipated the situation.

My dear Paul, I've struggled as liaison between you and the rest of the family for more than five years, gladly at times, and sorely at others. I've never seriously questioned your seclusion or your lifestyle...but now I realize how beneficial that isolation you so crave can be to the rest of us, how bearable your hermitage makes life for the rest of us.

Take care of yourself.

Susan

Runner

The pounding. Of his feet on the pavement. Of his breath in his chest. Of blood in his temples.

The pounding.

Trees and parked cars smear by as peripheral streaks of color. Sound volleys thunderously, a cacophony of street noise.

His eyes fix on the Hawthorne Building. Tiers of copper colored glass panes. Seven blocks to the corner, twice around the Hawthorne, three and a half miles back to the apartment.

The pounding.

Of air in and out of his lungs. Of the ache in his calves with each pace.

Red light…don't walk. Marking time, knees up, drip sweat. Green light…don't walk. Stride out.

Marcy, he thinks, is fat and soft. Not a runner. Marcy lopes, content to accept inertia rather than determine a pace. She does not lead.

Gresham Park, on the left, green slopes. Not for running. Grass yields, concrete responds. Run the streets, solid and disciplined.

Marcy knows no discipline, he thinks, she does not plan. She lacks forethought.

Sunlight, reflected off the Hawthorne, bronzes his body. Sweat blears his vision, whipped by the wind he creates against his face. He wipes his eyes and circles the final corner of the Hawthorne. Wave to the newsboy at the stand across the street.

Never has Marcy tested her limits. She does not realize she is limited because she has never tried her will. I love her, he thinks, but we are different people than before. Existing at different speeds.

He races over cloud shadows dappling the sidewalk. Another runner approaches head on, two blocks away. A young woman. Red satin shorts and a white shirt. Blue headband around brown hair. She is frowning, he notices, yet she is not straining herself. Her thighs are not lean. She has bad wind, he believes, as she draws closer. Her shirt is dry, and she smiles as she passes him.

That could have been Marcy, he imagines, but she will not even consider the run. She reads paperbacks while she reclines in the shade of the apartment balcony. "I exercise my mind," he hears her repeating. "While your body wastes," he counters.

No cramps. Two miles to go and no cramps. Slight discomfort in the lower back and a twinge behind the left knee. But good wind. Strong will. Easy distance and fine time. Run for time, not for distance.

"Just run for fifteen minutes with me," he has asked Marcy. "Don't worry about how far we'll go, just for fifteen minutes." She steadfastly refuses. He repeatedly admonishes her. We bicker, he thinks, but we coexist and share.

Next block is shopper's alley. Detour to the street. Asphalt of a texture more submissive than concrete. Dangers not so much from traffic as drivers opening doors of parked cars. A rainbow of roll-down awnings on his left, painted window signs, browsing walkers. A police siren wails through a side street and echoes as in a tunnel.

A city bus shoulders the curb, heated exhaust plumes around him as he passes. Noxious fumes, he thinks, rising high to the balcony, slowly staining the pages of Marcy's books.

The pounding.

Of urgency in his bowels. Of heat behind his eyes. Of his elbows chafing his sides.

His growing contempt for Marcy, though now mild, he admits, troubles him. Growth along parallel lines. But everyone knows parallel lines never meet. Not even on the horizon. He worries, but not gravely. Not with excessive concern.

Final mile, then check the pulse rate and walk. Home to Marcy. To the apartment. Pull open the drapes to scare away the dim mood of the living room. Shower under the hot water and steam relief into the tense muscles.

Marcy, he is sure, could learn to enjoy the effort, the race. A race not against time or distance, but against self. Ability versus faith. Frail endurance versus stalwart fatigue.

Sprint the last block, sidewalk cracks slide beneath his feet. His muscles scream. The poundings throb, like a drum staccato. Then he stutters to a walk, hikes his hands on his hips and heaves for cool air. He bends forward and sweat drops to the pavement. Half-mile walk, he thinks, then up the stairs to the apartment. Spare those on the elevator the taint of his pungency.

Everyone except Marcy. He smiles, more grimaces really, as he stretches to expand his lungs and fill them with air. Marcy deserves the full brunt of his odor. She warrants a tight embrace and a residue of slickness as he will pivot from her and trot to the bathroom. She will make a face and utter a sound of disgust. Then orange juice in a chilled glass waiting for him as he emerges from the shower.

The apartment building rises before him and he rings his apartment from the lobby. There is a pause then a buzzer drones. He pushes open the inner door and crosses to the stairwell.

Perhaps I should haul Marcy into the shower with me, he muses. Soap her down, then rinse her, and dry her with a bath towel. Carry her swaddled to the balcony.

The pounding.

Of his footsteps in the tall stairwell. Of his heart slowing in his chest. of his growing expectation of confronting Marcy.

The pounding.

He halts on the landing beside the door, which leads to his hallway, and once again checks his pulse rate. He smiles and opens the door. The carpet is another texture unsuitable for running.

The Seduction

Gary Bentley, readying his smile, that composite of probing eyes and toothy mouth, strode into the windowless room and halted by the chrome and plastic chair. To his right, on a divan yielding its stuffing to the carpet, sat a woman with hair the hue of coffee diluted with water. Her eyes were tender brown and she cradled her hands in the lap of her corduroy skirt, slender fingers tapering to unpainted nails. He instinctively knew they were the hands of a gentle woman. Small feet in chocolate-colored flats with imitation brass buckles; a sheer blouse over an intricately tatted lace camisole; faint traces of perfume, the fragrance animal and alluring. She side-glanced at Gary and he baited her with a grin, then sat in the chair, reserving the smile for a more providential moment.

The chairman of the creative writing program entered the room and advanced, waddling his bulk to the podium set against the front wall. He tapped the microphone with his pipe stem, Gary silently mouthing the words with him: "Is this thing on?" Feedback screeched through the rows of chairs, people snickered and the chairman adjusted the volume control on the console behind him. "Testing...testing. There, that's better. Welcome everyone."

Motion beside him distracted Gary as the woman clutched the hem of her skirt and fluidly crossed her legs.

"...and as a member of our faculty, Kenneth has distinguished himself, publishing a multitude of stories in various journals." Gary tilted his head back, counterfeiting an expression of grave concentration, while measuring the woman's face for any reaction to his sobering display.

"His novel, *The Topless Steak House*, should be released by Harmony Press this fall, and we're all hoping it'll be a critical and financial success, so that Kenneth will become more bearable around the office." A tittering of obsequious laughter from the chairman's students in the audience. "And so, without further ado, or unwarranted praise, ladies and gentlemen, Kenneth Praeger."

Gary applauded and scrutinized the woman on the divan, gauging her manner, alert for any hint, however oblique, that she had noticed him.

Kenneth Praeger moved to the podium, smiling without parting his lips. His flaring red beard salting to gray, ruddy taut skin and receding hairline, coupled with a shadow patch beneath his nose cast by the ceiling fixture directly above him, reminded Gary of a baboon's ass. Praeger shuffled his manuscript sheets and introduced his story.

"I suppose I should state that the idea, the inspiration as it were for this story, derives from an actual incident I witnessed one afternoon." Praeger spoke tonelessly, by rote, as though he had repeated the anecdote time and again until the mechanics of relating it had become automatic.

Gary glanced at the woman as she raised her hand and scratched her temple. If only she'd flutter those fingers through my hair, he thought, staring at her hands, wondering if their touch could ignite shivers like sparks.

"...and everything returned to some semblance of normalcy," Praeger continued. "Things don't occur that way in my story, as you'll soon learn, but the incident served to prick my imagination sufficiently to warrant the effort on these pages." Praeger clenched his sheaf in his hand and gestured at the crowd as though to baptize them. "The working title of the story is 'The Pleasures of Observation'."

So typical, Gary thought. The woman smiled briefly, affording Gary a glimpse of her teeth. My God! he thought, she's got an angelic mouth. What teeth. I wonder if she bites, just a teasing nip or two... the neck, the inside thigh, the lobe of my ear.

Praeger had begun. "...at the table, both of them mindlessly picking at the scraps of food on their plates. Her husband stared at the television screen, his face expressionless. She sighed and folded the cloth napkin in her lap, laying it across her plate of half-eaten food. She slowly pushed her chair back from the table, rose, and walked from the room. 'I'm going upstairs to take a bath,' she said to her husband without turning toward him."

She doesn't seem too terribly involved in the story, Gary pondered. She hasn't moved her head since Praeger began. It's no epic, but it's not entirely tranquilizing either. Oh, my God, he panicked, what if she's here to see Praeger! Praeger, Praeger, Praeger! The poor old sod, crumbling steadily into middle age like some aging cement wall. What can you see in him, my sweet? Gary glanced at the woman who sat stolidly, viewing Praeger with what Gary hoped was impassivity.

"...arresting her actions as she would an urge to scream in the face of stark terror." Praeger paused to sip juice from a violet ceramic mug.

The woman shifted in her seat; dust sifted from the slick worn upholstery as she ensconced herself upon the cushions and balanced her elbow on the arm of the sofa. Gary watched her, and grasping his moustache hairs gingerly between his thumb and forefinger, tugged downward, repeating the procedure again and again, hoping to dramatize for this sylph his pensiveness, his unfathomable depths of perception.

What name, he debated, could she dignify? Something whose very sound speaks of her gentility, her softness. Shari, perhaps, or Charlene. Maureen if it's breathed more than spoken. Or Heather, like meadow grass, easy and downey. Beth...Sarah...Lynn.

"...and steamed the bathroom mirror. She twisted the hot water tap until only cold water flowed into the tub. Then she wiped the condensation from the mirror and stared at her reflection: red eyes raw from crying. Her husband's footsteps scuffed on the stairs and she tightened the belt of her robe around her waist."

Oh, Praeger, Gary thought.

The woman turned her head and gazed in Gary's direction. He feared she had glanced beyond him, at a wall, a face, a chair.

I wonder, Gary speculated, if her performance would pay homage to her potential. That look! Those eyes! The manner in which she trains them on me like a sniper's scope. Passion would be instinctive and reflexive for her. The mattress is a canvas. Grazing her fingertips along my skin, delicately caressing the tiny hairs at the nape of my neck, rippling tides of sensational pleasure along my nerves like...well hell, like tremors on a fault line. My lord, what a devoted puppy I'd be for this bitch.

She sat rigidly with her back axle-straight against the sofa cushions as Praeger punctuated a prominent passage with a finger pointed at the audience.

"...and with her toes toyed with the chain attached to the drain plug. 'He was kind to me, as a friend,' she said, 'at a time when I was very vulnerable.' Seated on the toilet lid with her robe bundled at his feet, her husband ground the heel of one hand into the palm of the other. 'We had what I thought was a relationship based on trust,' he said. She closed her eyes and sharply inhaled, floating in the sudsy water."

A fluorescent tube in a lamp near the rear of the room flickered, flashing like a strobe, then darkened. Praeger's cadence floundered as he glanced up from his manuscript and scanned the room. Gary turned to view the woman. She had raised her head when the light flashed and her eyes held an expression of curiosity. Praeger cleared his throat, sipped from his mug of juice and continued reading. Gary contemplated the visage of the woman's face. Confidence, he reasoned, confidence and a surety of herself. Resolute. Oh yes, she's a level one all right.

I wonder if she likes it on top, Gary thought. I'll wager she loves wrapping her legs around her lover like a boa, pulling him to her until she feels as though she's been pierced. Uh huh. A siren, a wailer. At the very least a moaner and a clutcher. Clawing and raking, not ever getting enough, but God, giving so damned much. Passion...undiluted, unreined, untethered and unleashed. Ungodly. Unmarried? Damn, what if she's married? She's alone, after all. And maybe married. That would be so damned inconvenient.

"The bubbles from her bath gel had dissipated, and only clouded gray water remained in the tub as it colled. She lay in the water and turned her head to watch her husband. 'Marriage, I thought, meant exclusivity,' he said. 'But you obviously don't think so. You don't think so at all.' She felt the tension settle as a tightness in her temples. 'It's not the way you make it sound,' she complained. 'Nothing happened at all, and your own insecurities are forcing this situation. Damn it, I love you. Only you. Why can't you believe me? Why don't you want to believe me?'"

Honestly, Praeger, what drivel, Gary brooded. He fidgeted in his chair, wishing he had sat on the sofa, beside the woman, where his glances at her would not be as conspicuous. She must be tired of this claptrap Praeger's spewing, he thought, it's enough to anesthetize a deaf mute. Gary stretched his legs under the chair in front of him, arranging the heels of his boots beside one another, clapping the toes together in muffled thuds. Noticing the gossamer swirls of wispy hair in the hollow of her neck, Gary envisioned nuzzling his cheeks there while she purred and cooed, submissive and sated.

She can't be married, he thought.

"'I know,' she said, 'how it must have sounded to you. But who are you going to believe?' She gripped the edges of the tub and rose. 'Please hand me my robe.' He bent over and passed the robe to his wife. 'My job takes me out of town,' he began in an even voice. 'You know that, and it can't be helped. I don't think you fully appreciate how important coming home has been for me. I...' he stammered, 'I simply don't know what to believe when I get telephone calls like that.' He stood and faced his wife. She had wrapped herself in her robe and stood, staring at her reflection in the mirror."

Gary coughed and the woman swiveled her head to look at him. Jelly, he thought, I'm lounging here, being jellied by those big baby browns. Look at me, dear lord, look at me. Smile, won't you, he begged silently, smile at me and deign to grace me with your favors. Make me sweat and let that well-earned perspiration mingle with yours in one sweet moment of heaven. Jelly, jelly, jelly. Lance my nose and thread a ring through it. Lead me around, God, simply let me follow.

"He trailed her to the bedroom, where she sprawled on the bed, nestled her face in a pillow and quietly sobbed. 'Well, I just didn't know,' he said. 'Maybe it's like you said, I just don't want to confront this aspect of myself. I can be a jealous man, and this sort of thing really plays to that. Don't you understand?' he pleaded."

The woman reached beside the sofa and retrieved her hooded cape, draping it about her shoulders like a nun, an ordered creature of habit. Oh, don't cover that blouse, honey, Gary mused, you're too fine an object to be kept under wraps. Any wraps, even the wraps you're wearing now. I'd strip them from you like a peel, a section at a time, and watch the chill in the air ripple gooseflesh up and down your shapely form. Hah! Flesh, what an outstanding word! Fa...lesh! It sounds just as it should be. Flesh - as though you could submerge yourself in it; flesh - wallow in it; flesh - just lovingly revel in it.

"They lay beside one another on the bed, her head cradled in the hollow of his shoulder and neck. He stroked her hair gently as she slept, then covered them both with the bed sheet. He stared at the textured ceiling for some time, then deliberately closed his eyes and prayed for sleep."

Praeger ruffled his pages together and thanked the audience. Stuttered clapping then a more steady applause filled the room as people stood, flexing tired muscles. Gary also stood, stretching his arms before him with his hands linked, yawning deeply as he looked at Praeger absorbing people's praising comments like a vacuum. The woman rose and fastened her cape at the neck. Gary rooted himself at the end of the aisle and readied his smile. He was startled by a hand gripping his shoulder, steering him away from the woman.

"Well, Bentley," Praeger grinned fatuously, "what did you think of my tiny tale?"

"Oh, Kenneth," Gary said, maneuvering around Praeger, attempting to maintain the woman in his field of vision. "I thought the happy ending, such as it was, represented a departure from your usual."

The woman politely smiled at a tall man blocking her progress down the aisle, then sidled past him.

"But overall, the effect was...uh," Gary floundered as the woman paced to the rear of the room. "Uh...the effect was warming."

Gary watched as she seized the painted doorknob and twisted it in her hand.

"Very warming indeed," Gary said drolly as the woman opened the door and shrouded her head with the hood.

"Yes," Praeger readily agreed. "I thought so, too."

Cathedral

My father was baptized in the old cathedral, received his First Communion in the old cathedral, was confirmed in the old cathedral, and married my mother in the old cathedral. But today we celebrate his funeral in the new cathedral.

Nothing lasts forever.

My father disliked the new cathedral, with its polished wooden walls and high, square windows. Churches, he always said, should be built on and of stone; dark corners and stained glass windows, a haven where prayers would resound as in a cave. They should smell as old as religion and make anyone who enters feel just a bit afraid. For God was someone to fear.

My father was a pious man. He loved my mother and all her children. Before his illness he attended Mass daily, and visited his mother every other weekend except during Lent. It was never quite clear who gave up whom during that season.

His casket is gleaming blue metal, lined with cream-colored satin, and his gray-haired head rests on an elegant pillow such as was never seen on his bed. The gray suit he wore on Sundays has been pressed, and a tiny rosebud, which my sisters and I bought at the florist's shop yesterday, is pinned to his lapel. Father never cared for flowers, although at Easter he was the first to place a spray of lilies beside the altar before services. I do not believe he ever became comfortable watching the priest face him during Mass. He was a back watcher, more calm being guided than being confronted. I could never be content with that position, and our disagreement on this point and other progressive changes spanned more than a decade and a half. Our periodic arguments focused on ritualistic rather than theological points. To my father, the trappings were as important, if not more so, than the philosophy of his faith. God should not be as accessible as a civil servant, he professed. Mystery nurtured the faithful and disciplined them as a force for righteousness. His notions seemed archaic and served to cement the schism which had developed between us.

When I abandoned my engineering studies and entered the seminary in the early 1960s, my father's initial reaction was exhilaration. He gladly relegated his desire for grandchildren to my younger sisters, and lauded my vocation as a dream come true. The dream of every Catholic parent, to have a priest in the family.

I suppose my father's support during those years which culminated in my ordination represented his personal hope that I would single-handedly lead the wayward reformers back into the fold. Would reinject Latin into the Mass and restore that act to its former stature. Would once again shroud Catholicism in a cloak of indecipherable mysticism. He set himself up for the fall.

The bishop reassigned me to my home parish when my father's cancer was detected. Over dinner the first night home, this frail man quite obviously struggled with a dilemma. His adherence to tradition compelled him to decry what he perceived as the erosion of the Church, yet his instinctive awe of my collar and what it signified restrained him. He opted for a compromise, securing from me a vow that I would celebrate a requiem high Mass at his funeral. In Latin. The old way.

He was a persevering man. Perhaps our agreement, his victory of sorts, lessened the severity of his pain in these last days. He appeared more at ease than he had in years, knowing he had only to wait to relive the past.

The old cathedral has been demolished; the walnut pews and stained glass windows were auctioned off. Bought by strangers. And my father lies in state beneath the beams of blond wood in the new cathedral, as today we celebrate his funeral, his conquest of time.

The Invitation

The invitation, she realizes, arrives as confirmation of etiquette, since they agreed to part as friends; he does not intend for her to accept it and she cannot imagine attending the ceremony. Black Old English script on cream-colored paper textured to resemble parchment. The design lacks originality and she wonders if in the time since they last argued he has lost some of his spontaneity.

The bride's name is Oxner. What the hell, she muses.

Sitting at the secretary in the spare bedroom, she pens a short note of regret: best wishes...all possible happiness...previous engagement prevents.

Oxner. She wonders if the woman will retain her name.

From stacks of boxes in the dark closet beneath the basement stairs, she selects an appropriately-sized one and then another into which the first will nest. She then retrieves a ream of delicate tissue paper from one of the shopping bags which contain stored Christmas wrappings, some gold foil paper, and white ribbon.

She places the articles on the dining room table and walks to the Welsh dresser against the south wall, then lifts two hand cut crystal champagne glasses and carefully carries them to the table. The last of their champagne occasions together had been marked by a marginal misunderstanding which escalated and then exploded when he raised his hand as though to slap her; he had not, but the anger as it flickered across his features had engraved itself in her memory of him. Unwinding several sheets of tissue paper, she fashions a cradle in the smaller box and nestles the two glasses within the folds. She had not thought him capable of such malice, and although in retrospect the incident could not be said to have triggered their eventual uncoupling, it served to steer that course. From a drawer in the Welsh dresser she lifts a pair of silver scissors. They had sought and agreed upon a harmonious parting, a nearly surgical amputation of their affections for one another. With the flaps of tissue folded back from the edges of the box, she grips the scissors by the blades and strikes the handle down on the stem of one of the glasses. Phantom pain, it snaps cleanly.

She tucks the tissue around the crystal and closes the lid, then wraps the package in gold foil and circles it in white ribbon. Together with the note, she places the gift in the larger box, seals it with tape and addresses it to her.

Oxner. A toast to you both, she muses, may you touch one another as deeply as you have touched me.

Acknowledgments

"Grayson's Dreams" first appeared in *Four Quarters*, Volume 32, Number 4, Summer 1983.

"Koi Pond" first appeared in *Quick Fiction*, October 2004, and was reprinted in the inaugural issue of the *Bear River Review*, 2005.

"My Dear Paul," first appeared in the *Old Hickory Review*, Volume 12 Number 2 Fall/Winter 1980.

"Runner" first appeared in *Inside Running*, Volume 8 Number 3, March 1984.

"The Seduction" first appeared in Snapdragon, Volume 6 Number 2, Spring 1983.

"Cathedral" first appeared in the *Piedmont Literary Review*, Volume VII Issue II, 1982.

"The Invitation" first appeared in *Minotaur 7*, 1983, and was reprinted in *FlashFiction*, 2005-2006.

About the Author

JOHN M. MCNAMARA was born in New York City, and now lives in a suburb of Chicago. In the summer of 1999, he was selected to receive a professional artist residency at the Ox Bow Summer Arts Program for the School of the Art Institute of Chicago in Saugatuck, Michigan. He is the author of the novel **A LIFE WITHOUT GRACE.**

Made in the USA
Charleston, SC
24 March 2012